This book is published by Beach Holme Publishing, 226–2040 West 12th Avenue, Vancouver, B.C. V6J 2G2. *www.beachholme.bc.ca* This is a Porcepic Book.

The publisher gratefully acknowledges the financial support of the Canada Council for the Arts and of the British Columbia Arts Council. The publisher also acknowledges the financial assistance received from the Government of Canada through the Book Publishing Industry Development Program (BPIDP) for its publishing activities.

The Canada Council | Le Conseil des Arts
for the Arts | du Canada

BRITISH
COLUMBIA
ARTS COUNCIL
Supported by the Province of British Columbia

Editor: Michael Carroll
Cover Design: Herrainco | Skipp | Herrainco
Text Design and Production: Jen Hamilton
Cover Art: © Birgit Koch/firstlight.ca
Author Photograph: rarevisionphotography.com

Printed and bound in Canada by Houghton Boston

This is a work of fiction. Fiction may or may not be informed by personal experience. The characters and setting found within are imaginary composites and do not refer to actual persons or places. Any resemblance to actual or previously imagined places, factual or legendary events, real or seemingly real people, is purely coincidental and, of course, plausibly deniable.

National Library of Canada Cataloguing in Publication Data

Payton, Brian
 Hail Mary Corner

 ISBN 0-88878-422-8

 I. Title.
PS8581.A87H34 2001   C813'.6   C2001-911074-X
PR9199.4.P39H34 2001

HAIL MARY CORNER

HAIL MARY CORNER

Brian Payton

Porcepic Books
an imprint of

Beach Holme Publishing
Vancouver

For my father and mother

ACKNOWLEDGEMENTS

First and foremost, thanks are due to past, present, and future members of the UFSWEC. Thanks are also due to Barbara Bilsland, Tia Smith, and Andrew Greenwood for reading (and rereading) the earliest drafts; Michael Carroll for his dedication and editorial vision; Jim Skipp for his sense of style; Joan Clark, Edna Alford, and Michael Winter for encouraging words; and Trisha Telep for spreading the word.

Special thanks to my father for his example of faith and determination, and to Lily—for not counting the time it took to bring this story home.

What is time, then? If nobody asks me, I know; if I have to explain it to someone who has asked me, I do not know.

—St. Augustine (354–430 A.D.), *Confessions*

DEDICATION
September 1982

My knees were out of shape. It happened every summer. You spent all your time swimming, biking, lounging in the grass, and the callus that built up over the school year quickly wasted away. It was only when you came back in September that you remembered kneeling was supposed to be painful.

The new abbey church was filled with the soaring angelic polyphony of the seminarians and the haunting chant of the monks—Allegri's *Miserere mei*. Bowing my head and closing my eyes, I felt the presence of God. I could also feel the warmth of Jon kneeling next to me: a familiar whiff of soap and evaporating Aqua Velva.

When I opened my eyes, I saw the greasy scalps of seminarians gently bobbing in front of me, and black monks displayed in neat rows in the oak stalls to the left. Across from us in the north transept sat a cardinal and three bishops in pointy mitres, plus a pair of short Orthodox abbots with nearly identical salt-and-pepper beards. On the right a capacity crowd of regular priests, nuns, and laypeople filled the nave to overflowing. In the centre stood a massive granite altar under the curve of a dome sixty feet in the air. Late-morning sunlight streamed through stained glass, bathing the pallbearers in red, orange, and yellow as they entered the aisle in the middle of the faithful.

Four seminarians from the senior class carried a small box atop a wooden litter draped in a shawl of white with a gold cross on top. Stiff and serious, they stopped at the foot of the altar where the abbot and four monks in gold-brocade vestments waited with the cardinal, who tipped his crosier—the hooked staff of the Shepherd of Men—in solemn consent. With wizened hands the monks reached out and took the box from the boys, nodded a blessing to them, then placed it carefully under the altar.

The box contained the relics of Saint Scholastica, patroness of rain. She was invoked against childhood convulsions. Her greatest claim to fame, however, was the fact that she was the twin sister of Saint Benedict. Under every altar there should be buried some holy thing: blobs of dried blood, hair, body parts, or personal effects. In this case, we were told, it was bones. I closed my eyes again and wondered what kind of bones were in that little box. Jaw? Teeth? Skull cap? Probably her knees, I thought, feeling my own go numb.

I was late again this year, my third at the Seminary of Saint John the Divine. I had arrived just in time to jump out of my shorts and into wool pants and a navy blazer—our school uniform. The organ called out to me as I frantically changed, alone, all the way up in the juniors' dorm. I tied my tie as I ran to the ceremony, the familiar clomp of last year's shoes echoing through the hall.

The monks had been waiting for this "D-Day" since long before we were born. A model of the planned church had been gathering dust in the guesthouse lobby since 1957. What they ended up with looked completely different.

The new abbey church was a sprawling concrete edifice with a pointed dome. It had dozens of tall, abstract, stained-glass windows, a rainbow of cough drops melted together. From the outside it appeared as if a giant spaceship had landed from some postmodern Catholic galaxy. It took three and a half years to build—a good part of it with seminarian slave labour—and like the great churches of old, it would probably never really be finished. Father Ezekiel, our ancient, liver-spotted science teacher, said the new structure would stand at least until 2482, barring nuclear attack.

As the *Miserere* faded, the cardinal called for the Holy Spirit. "Come down and bless this place," he said. "Make it a sanctuary dedicated to the worship of God from this day forward." I closed my eyes again and imagined the Holy Spirit descending from the popcorn clouds, through the flatulent stench of the pulp-mill town. He'd see the church, the monastery, and the seminary lined up along the cliff—the bell tower like a beacon leading him in. He'd pass through the thick concrete dome and hover over the altar where the cardinal and monks raised the Blessed Sacrament to the sky. He'd breathe in the rich incense and know he was home. I opened my eyes. There was no sign of the Holy Spirit. Instead, when the organ fell silent and the cardinal stopped mumbling, we all heard a sound very much of this world.

Every head turned to the back of the church where a huge baptismal font bubbled holy water over granite rocks and into a little pool. The cardinal paused a moment more to make sure of what he heard. *Crock, crock* echoed again, announcing the fact that an amphibian had taken up residence in God's newest house. The place erupted in applause.

"It sounds as if all the earth is celebrating today," the cardinal said. "All God's creatures are raising their voices in praise."

When I was a child, I wanted to be a priest. I wanted to be the lightning rod for all that limitless spiritual power. I would walk down the street knowing that the saints and angels were backing me up and that I was doing the most important thing in this world: God's Work. That was, after all, why we were here. And so I left home for the seminary.

Perched high above Vancouver Island's broad Ennis Valley, the Seminary of Saint John the Divine was a boarding school with a specific agenda: to help young men find their Calling and to aid in their Priestly Formation. Everyone, right down to the scrawniest, snot-nosed freshman, had to give a rating of his potential religious vocation on a scale of one to ten. "One" meant you were probably an atheist and "ten" signalled candidacy for canonization. It happened at the beginning of each term. I always rated myself a respectable "six"—high enough to show a spiritual pulse but low enough to avoid any undue attention. But as time went by and increasing doses of testosterone pulsed through my veins, it was becoming abundantly clear I wasn't cut out for the job.

Saint John the Divine was run by monks; Benedictines to be exact. Their kind had been living the Rule of Saint Benedict since *anno domini* 529. Their wardrobe consisted of identical black-hooded habits. They eschewed vanities like deodorant and toothpaste— baking soda was good enough. Shampoo was for women.

Until I actually came across one I had a storybook idea of monks. Friar Tuck and the Grim Reaper instantly sprang to mind. The first one I ever encountered was Brother Thomas. A tall, skeletal man slightly older than my father, he had a permanent squint as if he'd been sucking a lemon or was thinking so hard he was about to burst a blood vessel.

"Man of God!" he declared that very first day as he surveyed my *Rocky III* T-shirt and tight blue jeans. I hadn't even made it into the building. The earphones attached to a poorly concealed Walkman were of particular interest. Carefully he removed them from my head and listened to Billy Idol for a moment before issuing his signature grimace. He told me to change out of my "getup," then store it and the offending machine in my trunk. "Be on time and in uniform for the Reading of the Rules," he added. "There the Veil of Misunderstanding will surely be lifted."

This morning, this Dedication Day, Brother Thomas stood unnaturally erect in front of his stall "conducting" the *schola*, his hand undulating like a belly dancer's over his Latin *graduale*. No one paid him any attention.

Father Albert was my second monk. He was a plump, rose-cheeked man of considerable style and charm. After my name and where I was from, the next thing he wanted to know about me was the last movie I'd seen. Addicted to films, Father Albert confessed he hadn't been out to a theatre since *Doctor Zhivago*. He survived on videos and detailed accounts of recent movies from his students. I was to tell him all about *Star Trek: The Wrath of Khan*.

Today, for this momentous occasion, Father Albert was seated at the helm of his new pipe organ, eyes closed, arms outstretched, head thrown back in ecstasy.

"*Amplius lava me ab iniquitate mea, et a peccato meo munda me*," we sang. Wash me clean of my guilt, purify me from my sin.

On the way back from Communion I stopped to take it all in. I nearly tripped looking up at the distant honeycombed ceiling, then followed Jon into our pew where we knelt and made the sign of the cross in perfect unison. As I watched Father Albert sweat and sway toward a musical crescendo, the Eucharist attached itself firmly to the roof of my mouth. I held it there with my tongue until it dissolved like an M&M and became part of me, body and soul.

As I prayed, I thought about my grandfather. He had died that summer, and every day since I had been variously haunted or comforted by the knowledge that he was now omniscient, gazing down from heaven, watching my every move. He saw me here, kneeling at the dedication of the new abbey church, and he was proud. But he also saw me when I was naked, playing with myself in the shower before I left on the bus for the seminary. I was nearly paralyzed with guilt after that, knowing in my heart that he saw what these hands, these same hands that were pressed together in prayer, had been doing only two days before.

So, I prayed to my grandfather, *now you know the truth*.

During that endless Mass, I had time for a revelation. If my grandfather was in heaven, how could he be upset or disappointed? Wasn't he shielded from all things unpleasant in the radiant face of God? It seemed a terrible fate to have to watch people for eternity picking their noses, stealing, and doing and thinking all the other things they did and thought in private. This led me to wonder about the saints, the angels, and even God Himself: all of them watching us fall and beg forgiveness, fall and beg again. Down here we only had full knowledge of our private lives. We only truly knew our sinful selves. I thought what an unbearable burden it must be to know the sins and secrets of all the world, especially the ones you loved.

☥

The afternoon sunlight pushed down on Saint John the Divine like a hand on the back of a neck. But with the blue-sky backdrop and green junipers out front the place looked like a postcard from somewhere a whole lot better than this.

Although it was Monday, we had the day off. The monks had another big Mass with the remaining bishops, abbots, and assorted Catholic wheels. The party atmosphere died down right after lunch as the guests finally left the monks and student body to settle into their new/old routines.

Saint John's was a simple three-story structure of bare grey cinder blocks and big picture windows. A terra-cotta roof flattered it with the look of an old California mission. The seminary wing was connected to the monastery by way of the scullery, dining halls, and guesthouse. The gentle side of the hill rolled down from the buildings and the new abbey church in a quilt of sun-bleached grass, lush clover, and dandelions past their prime. It came to an indeterminate end at a small body of water at the edge of the woods and the foot of Mount Saint John.

The monks preferred us to call it Mary Lake, but that would be overly kind. About fifty yards across and only eight feet deep in the middle, it was semi-square, betraying its man-made origins. The pond attracted boys, frogs, and flies and exuded a fetid stink during the warmest months. Its ill-defined banks were slick with mud, and it was difficult to tell where land ended and water began. To the student body it had always been and would forever remain the Bog.

Dandelion seeds cartwheeled down the hill and brushed against my ankles. Cool clay oozed between my toes. Jon floated on his back, arms splayed, fingers moving enough to keep him afloat on the smooth, almost stagnant surface.

Although we had exchanged letters and the odd phone call,

we'd gone nearly three months without seeing each other and, to me, that seemed like forever. I wondered if he felt the same.

Jon had changed since I'd last seen him. His face was slightly more angular than before, jaw more pronounced. His shoulders appeared wider. Over the summer he had even grown a few curly black hairs on his sternum. I glanced down at my bare chest, then dived in, disturbing the calm. Staying under until my lungs burned, I resurfaced behind him. "Miss me?" I asked.

He lied and said he didn't, then silently slipped away, tea-coloured skin flowing easily under the surface, the dark waves of his hair smoothed flat against his skull. He couldn't stay under as long as I could. After coming up and gasping for breath, he rubbed his eyes and stared at the new abbey church. "What do you think about all that money going for a building like that? It's not like any poor people will ever get the chance to use it."

I swiped the hair from my eyes and blew my nose. "When you say stuff like that, it makes me think you're reacting against your own cushy life. You wanna hang with the poor people? Come on over to my place for a while."

Jon's family owned Benning Home Furnishings: *Quality & Tradition Since 1953*. He always had a selection of new shoes and, other than his school uniform, he never wore the previous year's clothes. On top of being rich, Jon had "class"—a kind of charm and refinement I was beginning to notice in others but found sorely lacking in myself.

Blessed with dark, deep eyes, Jon also had skin that was always a shade or two healthier than mine. When he smiled, people stopped what they were doing. From visiting sisters to the girls at the corner store, the few women who entered our lives were united in their opinion: hearts would be broken. Even my own mother said as much. Jon and I really didn't look much alike—me being pale, my hair straight and blond—but sometimes when we were in town people would mistake us for brothers. That always made me proud.

Jon filled his mouth with Bog water and spat it at me in a thin stream through perfect white teeth. "I guess I did miss you."

Relief flowed warmly inside me. We floated together, suspended in the last few moments of freedom. Tomorrow classes would start and the whole heavy, antique machinery of the place would shake and rumble to life, then hum all the way to Christmas.

An indistinguishable black form emerged from the guesthouse two hundred yards away. We both squinted, unable to determine who it was. But when the hands went up and rested on the hips, we knew we were regarding Father Albert. He stopped and watched us floating in the Bog, staring back at him. Looking left and right down the empty drive, he started marching across the field.

The first thing to come off was his scapular—over his head and onto the grass. Then came the belt. He picked up the pace and unbuttoned his habit, shrugging it off halfway to the Bog and continuing his waddling jog in T-shirt, boxers, black socks, and shoes. Jon and I turned to each other, bug-eyed with surprise, ready to laugh but not knowing where to begin. Then off came the shoes and socks and finally, at the edge of the mud, the extra-large T-shirt. Skin that white shouldn't be exposed to the elements.

"You're the man, Pair!" Jon cried, nearly climbing out of the water. "You *are* the man."

When the other monks weren't around, we called him Pair because *père* was French for *father* and he hated teaching French; because he was shaped like a pear; and because he did things no other monk would do.

"Watch out for the tsunami, boys." He displaced a surprisingly small amount of water, then floated on his back, his taut, hairless gut breaching the surface like the head of a beluga. Treading water with unnatural ease, he murmured, "Isn't it great when you wait for something, wait a really long time, and it turns out better than you imagined? Must be a little like heaven." He rolled off his back and scanned the hill to ensure the coast was still clear, then gazed up past the trail of clothes to the new abbey church. "It's not every day the world gets such a magnificent new sanctuary. I feel like a kid again."

I sighed, then dog-paddled a figure eight around to the two of them. "It's just a fancy room for a pipe organ."

Father Albert's eyes narrowed slightly, then shifted in my direction. As a satisfied smile stretched across his face, he blew bubbles in the Bog and laughed. "Pinch me. I must be dreaming."

※

Night in the dorm. The juniors' dorm now, not the nursery. The freshmen and sophomores were down the hall, crammed together in the biggest room on campus. Although it was more permanent and less crowded, the nursery reminded me of one of those gymnasium disaster relief centres you see on television with people flaked out all over the floor after an earthquake or flood. Even in the relatively posh juniors' dorm we slept side by side, partitioned off by flimsy chin-level dividers. Privacy was for people with something to hide.

The bed cradled me hammocklike on old sagging springs. Breathing in bleach, sweat, and dust off the sheets and thin mattress, I could see the lump of Jon in the bed across from me, with Saint Charles Borromeo staring down from his frame on the wall above. Connor, the other guy in our bay, had nailed St. Chuck up there. Aside from being the patron of seminarians, the saint, like Connor, suffered from a debilitating stutter. I couldn't see him clearly in the dark, halo radiating around his piously cocked head, but I was aware of his gaze. Then someone whimpered in his sleep and I began to pray.

Five days, Lord, and holding. Help me keep my promise to turn away from sin. Help me fight myself and never give up. Make me strong. Make me strong. Make me...

I listened to our breathing. We all seemed to fall into a pattern. Finally I drifted away on a stream of Hail Marys, travelling away from myself, away from what was into what would never be.

TWO

ROMANS AND CHRISTIANS

The close September evening gave no hint of the coming change of season. On its way down, the setting sun kissed the nipple of rock at the top of the large, full hill that was Mount Saint John. When the day finally slipped past the edge of the horizon, the last of the light pooled in the Bog in a blue-orange sheet like metal exposed to fire.

I wasn't sure how they played it at other schools, but at the Seminary of Saint John the Divine, contestants concentrated on the apprehension, torture, and simulated martyrdom of Christians. Most boys wanted to be Roman.

Old foxholes were dug in the black forest soil. They had been there for generations, hidden behind bushes and under the fan of upturned trees. Everyone knew where they were, except the new kids. I stood alone inside one such crater, last year's leaves rotting in a pool at my feet. It smelled like urine. I could hear hoots and hollers spread thin in the distance. Crouching down, I pulled out a

Marlboro, tapped it on the crush-proof box, and lit it. Jon jumped in from out of nowhere and splashed some of the muck on my cheek.

"*Scrupus*," I said, lighting the cigarette, then wiping my face.

"*Nutrix*," Jon replied.

"Where's Connor?" I asked.

"Dunno."

"What's the plan?" I took a long drag and tried to look like an army field officer discussing plans for an offensive.

"Eric's a Christian," Jon announced. "Volunteered again."

"He's so literal. He'll go far." There was a rustling of leaves and then choked laughter from behind a rotting log. We both heard it. I removed the cigarette, put a finger to my lips, and winked. "So maybe we'll head back toward the gym," I said just loud enough for them to hear.

"Yeah. We'll surprise the little shits down there."

Jon pulled my head close and whispered in my ear that he'd leave, making enough commotion for both of us. I should stay behind for the ambush. As soon as he heard me yell, he'd come flying back. I gave him a drag, pinched off the half-smoked butt, and replaced it in the deck. Jon disappeared into the quiet.

Half an hour earlier I had fished a folded little slip of paper with an *R* out of a baseball cap, which meant I got to hunt down passive apostles and bring them to justice. Roman justice. That should have been exciting, but I was getting a little too old for this kind of crap.

A few minutes later the new kids poked their noses over the rim of the foxhole and peered in. Fresh veal. I scrambled up the side of the hole, slipping and landing on my shin as they hopped away like deer. Jon saw them. He was waiting behind the trunk of an immense maple. We tore after them full-tilt.

Trunks whizzed by in the blue-black twilight. We were closing in. When they were almost to the edge of the Bog, one of them whined like a dog about to get whacked with a broom.

Jon already had his Christian subdued. In mid-stride I reached out just as my man turned around to see. I grabbed him by the collar and we both instantly tripped, tumbling over the mossy twigs into the tall grass. Quickly I jumped back up, hands in front of me ready to choke. The kid lay frozen on his face hoping that if he played dead long enough I might just sniff him, paw around, then wander back into the woods for some berries.

"Get up!" I ordered.

"I'm sorry," he mumbled straight into the ground.

"Sorry for what? Getting caught? Now you're going to die for your faith." I took out the now-crumpled deck of smokes and lit one.

"Who are you?" he asked, slowly sitting up.

"Who am *I*?" I blew smoke down at him.

"You never came to the Reading of the Rules."

"Who am *I*? That should be one of the first things you learn here."

"Sorry."

"Stop with the sorry routine. Get up."

He stood. I couldn't see him well, but he was a small kid with wide hips and narrow shoulders like those of a girl. His skin seemed pasty, his eyes were almond-shaped, and he had thin, serious lips. You couldn't really tell if he was white or Mongolian or some wild mix of the two.

"The question," I said, "is who the hell are you?"

"Michael Ashbury."

He didn't look like an Ashbury, that was for sure. I grabbed his collar again, blew a puff of smoke into his face, then shoved him toward the Coliseum. Jon was already leading his Christian down the Appian Way, and I was falling behind.

❋

Mosquitoes filled the air. I almost breathed one in. The Bog churned them out like a factory. There were three flashlights among thirty seminarians. The others were still in hiding or pursuit, and we couldn't wait any longer. Rosary was only fifteen minutes away.

Connor had a Christian down on his knees. It was Dean, a member of our own class. A couple of other guys lit candles and placed them in a half circle behind him.

Physically Dean was completely average; intellectually he was right off the scale. The results of an IQ test he had taken the year before were so impressive that colleges and universities were already calling the monks from as far away as England. The actual score was a tightly held secret.

Dean was one of those guys who could be cool one minute, moody and withdrawn the next. We tried letting him hang out with us for a while the previous year, but he didn't have much to say. He was too wrapped up in his own thing, so we let him slip back into obscurity. Now, in the flashlight beam, Dean folded his arms and rolled his eyes.

Connor Atkins was also intelligent, but he shone as the natural athlete of our class. He filled out faster and better than the rest of us. There was an eternal energy about Connor—the way he moved in bold, fluid gestures. He seemed anxious at rest, fully realized in motion. Because of his stutter, he felt more articulate using the language of his body.

Rolling up the sleeve of his T-shirt, Connor made an impressive muscle. Even in the candlelight we could see the glint in his blue eyes and the green vein on his hard right biceps.

"I'm shaking," Dean said, putting his hands on his hips.

"Say 'Hail Caesar' or j-j-join the s-saints," Connor ordered.

"Hmm. How 'bout 'Fuck you' instead?"

Everyone gasped. Connor smiled, turned as if he was going to let it go, then pushed Dean onto his ass and into the candles. The Romans went wild.

"G-g-get in l-line," Connor commanded.

Dean got in line with the four other Christians, then I pushed mine down on the shoulder until he was kneeling in the candles. Standing in front of him, I cracked my knuckles and said, "I don't want this to get ugly."

The kid instantly burst into tears. He sat in the dirt and covered his face as Eric arrived on the scene. "Bill! What did you do to him?" Eric pushed people aside to get at me. "You're not supposed to hurt anybody."

Eric Dumont had an overly developed sense of right and wrong. He was the most religious kid I had ever met—forever trying to recruit people into the Knights of Mary or some other holy society. He wasn't really effeminate, but he had the long, slender hands of a woman and was always meticulously groomed. Eric's hair was his favourite feature. It never yielded to gravity or wind. Dishwater-brown, it was always parted in the middle and flipped back over his ears, Bee Gees–style, and lacquered in place with mousse and hair spray which, along with all hair products, were illegal at Saint John the Divine. He forgave himself this transgression. Sometimes to mask an acne rash growing in that slick, shiny area of his forehead, he'd comb half his bangs down and zap them in place with an extra dose of hair spray that made him look even more ridiculous. We had always been friends, Eric and I, but sometimes I wondered how it all had happened in the first place.

"I didn't do anything!" I said. "I didn't even lay a finger on him."

Eric was right. The first day of class and I had humiliated this kid in front of half the school. The other half would know before their heads hit their pillows. I apologized, then reached out my hand. He took it. I pulled him up and tried to force a smile, but it was much too late.

"It's just a game," I said. "I didn't—"

"Line 'em up." Connor took control, and Michael Ashbury fell in with the other Christians. One of the Romans looked at his watch and announced it was ten minutes to rosary. We formed the gauntlet.

Each Christian was given the final chance to say "Hail Caesar." One of the freshmen caved in and was set free to live in shame. The others were then pushed one by one between two rows of Romans who slapped and shoved, cursed and cuffed the Christians as they passed through. Most put their heads down and ran, receiving little real damage. Eric walked in a slow, dramatic procession, head held high, letting each of us get two or three shots in before he reached the end.

When it came to my Christian, I looked away. I wanted him to have a chance to say his "Hail Caesar" without making it worse than I already had. But Michael Ashbury took a deep breath, let out a weird little laugh, and charged through the Romans. I gave him a cuff on the back of the head, but not too hard. Just enough to let him know I wasn't babying him.

✳

An almost life-size crucifix loomed over the altar in the student chapel. It was abstract, in the style of the 1960s. Carved from white marble, it looked as much like a mummy or a cocoon as a replica of our Lord in agony. In the back corner of the chapel a more normal statue of the Blessed Virgin stepping on a serpent kept watch over us from behind. A solitary kneeler was parked directly in front of Our Lady's feet. Eric often said his rosary there. On three of the four walls were the Stations of the Cross below a row of small square windows. The windows were up high and made of coloured, textured glass like the kind found in washrooms and other places where people shouldn't look in.

There, on its knees under the fluorescent lights, the student body mumbled through never-ending prayers. Each one served to remind me I was straying farther from a state of grace. The Finger of God, it seemed, was pointed directly at me, and I cursed all parents who had christened their daughters Mary.

"Hail, Mary, full of grace, the Lord is with thee. Blessed art thou among women and blessed is the fruit of thy womb, Jesus..."

Mary O'Brien was a local girl whose family came to Mass every Sunday morning. She had spent her entire life below the cliff in Ennis, the bell tower and Mount Saint John her inescapable points of reference. Toward the end of the previous year we started going on walks together. I made her laugh; she gave me impure thoughts. This sort of "fraternization" had to be kept away from school grounds. The monks couldn't have us "strolling up and down the drive with every girl in town." I guess they had more faith in our ability to be desired by local representatives of the opposite sex than we did.

The Sunday before the end of the spring term Mary and I had stolen away to the path behind the Bog. We ended up on the bench in front of the secluded statue of Our Lady of the Lake, a place created for quiet, holy meditation. She sat smiling on the bench in the dappled maple light. My hand wasn't exactly up her blouse, but I could see how it might have looked that way from a distance. We were making out, I admit, but Brother Thomas wasn't interested in hearing my defence.

"Holy Mary, Mother of God, pray for us sinners now and at the hour of our death. Amen."

The rosary was made up of three groups of five Mysteries each. The second group, the Sorrowful Mysteries, included events in the Lord's journey through the streets of Jerusalem on His way to crucifixion. We took turns reading the brief descriptions out of the prayer book about how Saint Veronica wiped the face of Jesus or how Simon of Cyrene shouldered the cross for a few steps. You were supposed to dedicate each Mystery to some pressing international concern: the conversion of the Soviet Union, the relief of the famine in Ethiopia, or world peace were all acceptable selections. Then it was Michael Ashbury's turn to take the lead. We juniors were kneeling five pews back, so all I could see was his skinny little neck.

"I wish to dedicate the next Mystery to the upperclassmen at Saint John's," he said. "For more maturity in certain juniors and seniors so they won't pick on kids smaller than them this year. Hail, Mary, full of grace..."

At the end of rosary Jon nudged my shoulder and gestured to the stairwell where Father Gregory was beckoning me. I squeezed out of the pew and genuflected toward the Blessed Sacrament. Then Father Gregory led me down the empty hallway past the open classrooms, the hem of his habit fluttering nervously behind him.

Father Gregory was the rector or headmaster of the seminary. That meant our day-to-day welfare was in his hands. He was our surrogate parent/prison guard. He was also a serious man who had about twelve doctorates and who read the Latin version of the Bible—with the Greek and Hebrew cross references in the margins—just for fun.

He had bad dandruff, and it collected on the inside of his glasses in a filthy haze. Trying to establish eye contact with him was frustrating. I wanted to take his glasses off, wipe them on his habit, then put them back on his face so I could see him better. Let's just say he wasn't one of those monks you could imagine boozing it up with Robin Hood and the Merry Men after hijacking the king's coach. Besides, he was too old—at least 108, it seemed. He often mentioned living through eight popes in much the same way other old people talked about having survived both world wars. But despite his age he was strong and imposing. He was still over six feet tall.

Father Gregory's office was known as the Cave. Although it was right off the foyer in the heart of the seminary, we rarely had cause to enter. It was both intimidating and exotic. This was the place your dad came on Parents' Day and sat with you across the desk from Father Gregory. It was here that you suddenly realized your old man was almost as afraid as you were.

The door to the Cave opened on a long, narrow hallway that led to a dimly lit office with about two thousand books covering grey stone walls. Only half of the titles were in English. Everything was neat, dusted, and in its place. The only thing betraying human habitation was a newspaper tossed a little haphazardly onto the Naugahyde couch. Presiding sorrowfully over everything was a big Russian icon of the Madonna and Child.

Behind Father Gregory's teak desk was a large window that looked out onto the middle of a colossal rhododendron that had grown into a small forest. The Cave was on the main floor of the seminary, and the dormitory wing above—particularly the window over the sinks in the washroom—could be clearly seen from my seat. I knew Jon, Connor, and Eric were probably up there with the lights turned out, watching us and making up dialogue as they saw my lips move. I tried to keep from looking.

"How are you settling in this year?" Father Gregory had my file out. It, and an antique fountain pen, were the only things on the desk. Every seminarian had one of these neat dossiers with lists and dates and records of everything you'd ever done or were likely to do. He hovered over a page, scratched something in there with his old pen, then finally looked up, waiting for my answer.

"Uh, fine. I guess."

"Doesn't sound very definitive to me."

"Great. Everything's great."

"Have you had time to put any more thought toward your vocation?"

At the end of the previous year I was invited not to return to Saint John the Divine. The inventory of reasons included attitudinal problems, a questionable dedication toward a religious vocation, a general lack of respect, a tendency to incite rebellion, and the "liaison" with Mary. I was given the summer to pray, think things through, search my heart, and try to come to some conclusion about whether I should return for my third year a "new man" or stay at home and make the best of public school.

"I'm back, aren't I? I want to be back."

Father Gregory scribbled something else. "Where do you see yourself in ten years?" It was the priesthood question in another guise.

"Well, maybe teaching religion someplace like Rwanda. Maybe I'll become a Jesuit." The monks hated the Jesuits, only they couldn't admit it. We said things like this just to make them mad. "But I'm not even a senior yet. Who knows what they're going to be when they're sixteen?"

He squinted a little, then leaned back in his cushy chair. Shadows moved in the washroom window above his head. "Don't you miss your family and friends back in Calgary?"

Well, actually, my only friends were interred here on Saint John's thousand acres. Father Gregory knew that. The group I had grown up with back home had gone off in such entirely different directions that I hardly had anything to say to them. My brother and sisters were all off in their own lives, busy putting our family behind them. For some reason much was expected from parents who'd done almost nothing themselves. My mother worked at the Calgary "International" School of Beauty. My father, a postal worker and regional union representative, believed in progress and often said he'd be damned if he was going to let his kids grow up to sort mail or tint hair.

"No one expects you to take vows yet," Father Gregory said.

"We're already living a life of poverty, chastity, and obedience, aren't we?"

He smiled, took a deep breath, and carefully placed the pen on the file. Locking his gaze between my eyes, he dared me to look away. "Let's be specific. Do you see yourself as a brother or a priest?"

I hesitated only for a moment. I felt I could trust him. "I don't know, Father. Were you absolutely sure when you were my age?"

"Fifty-two years ago—1930—I was your age. I was living at St. Cuthbert's Abbey in New Brunswick, and there was nothing I wanted more in the world than to become a priest."

He rested his hands on the desk and looked over my head at the ceiling, thinking back half a century. I glanced above his head and through the darkness, squinting into the third-story washroom window, certain I could see something move. The lights came on and there they were, waving, jumping up and down, making faces. Then the lights went out again.

"My parents were killed in a train wreck when I was eleven," Father Gregory said without the slightest hint of emotion. "My sister was sent to a convent and I was sent to the abbey. The monks raised me to love God and to listen to Him, to listen for a calling. But from my earliest recollection I knew I'd become a priest. I also wanted to become a professional baseball player, mind you, but I knew that wasn't in the cards... So, no, I don't think it's outside the realm of possibility for a young man your age to have some inkling God may be calling him."

This was the offer of a fresh start, the hand of friendship extended. It was my chance to suck it up, to submit. But something inside me wouldn't let it happen.

"Did you ever think, even for a second, that the death of your parents had something to do with your decision to become a monk?" I asked. "You practically grew up in a monastery. I mean, it wasn't a normal childhood. And maybe if your parents had lived..."

He didn't say anything, just stared at me. Then he bent over and wrote something in the file, paused again, noted something else, flipped it closed, and pushed it aside.

"I mean, I see your point, with your story and all, but—"

He raised his hand to stop me from making it worse. "This is a pivotal year for you, William. A pivotal semester. We're here to show young men what a religious life is like, to help them find their vocation. That's what this place is all about. It's a seminary, not a cheap boarding school. You have some more thinking and praying to do." He gestured toward the door. "Join your confreres, but understand, you won't be indulged any longer. You're a young man. Being a man means having to make decisions. I'll pray for you. Please pray for me."

※

At 12:07 a.m. the sound of a distant splash made it all the way to the open window of our dorm. I heard it again, then some murmuring. It was coming from the Bog. I slipped out of bed and tiptoed to the window.

To keep the world out and our attention in, the dorm windows started six feet off the floor. I stood on a chair and leaned on the cool tile sill. The butternut tree blocked most of the view, but I could just make them out through the crook of a bare branch. It took my eyes a while to adjust, but when they did I saw five or six silhouettes in the half-moon light. They were too far and too dark to make anything out, but I knew they were freshmen. There was a pause, a small splash, someone speaking, then silence. I had to hold my breath and cup my ears to hear anything. When it happened the third time, I remembered. They were being baptized tonight, and Michael Ashbury would be among them.

Aside from Romans and Christians, which everyone played, new seminarians didn't undergo systematic hazing at Saint John the Divine. They were baptized instead. I heard another splash and remembered my own Bog baptism two years before. The ritual was always performed by sophomores and had been going on almost as long as the seminary itself. Unlike the current evening and its heat wave, that night was cool and cloudy. I stood in the muck up to my knees in almost total darkness and listened to the words—a not-so-clever send-up of the Apostles' Creed.

"Do you believe in Saint John's and the Spirit of the Sem?"

The kid in front of me, the one about to get pushed underwater, said, "I do."

"Do you believe in loyalty, courage, bravery, and truth?"

He did.

"Do you believe in the sacred brotherhood in which you are about to share?"

That, too.

"Do you believe in seeking, supporting, fomenting, and aiding REDRO at all times and under all circumstances?"

He nodded.

"Then I say, Spirit of the Sem, come down on this man and make him one of us this day and forever more." Here the initiate's head was pushed underwater and held there while the sophomore pronounced, "I baptize you in the spirit of REDRO." He made a counterclockwise circle in the air with his left hand as everyone answered a hushed amen.

REDRO was our call to anarchy. REDRO was the mission to pull at the loose threads wherever they were found, to resist in ways big and small, to undermine the monks' total control. REDRO was about fighting for everything boys had a right to be. REDRO was ORDER spelled backward.

When it was my turn, I listened to the words refract underwater, the cool blackness enveloping me completely. It seemed to go on forever, and my only tie with the surface was the hand holding my head down firmly. Eventually I panicked and pushed upward, trying to reach the air. But I just sank farther into the mud. The boy at the other end of the hand was now silent, and by the time the amen finally reached my ears, he was already lifting me up by my jersey, pulling me back from the murky water an entirely new man.

"What are you doing, pervert?" Eric demanded, interrupting my recollection. He was standing behind me in his pajamas, arms folded across his chest. Jon stood behind him, rubbing his eyes.

"Baptisms tonight," I said.

"No, freak. Why are you standing there naked?"

I wasn't naked—I was wearing underwear—but at Saint John the Divine the absence of pajamas constituted nudity.

"You'll get in trouble. Again." Eric hopped onto the chair beside me and looked past the butternut tree, thinking no doubt of his own freshman baptism. Jon waited until I stepped down, then took my place on the chair with Eric to watch the last kid get dunked. But the pair soon shuffled off to bed and the dorm was quiet once again.

I heard the cellophane flap of dragonflies through the open window. It reminded me of when I was a kid chasing fireflies down at my grandfather's house in Texas. I thought that if I could find one this far north I'd catch it, tie it to a little loop of string, and slip it glowing down Mary's finger by the moonlit Bog. She was the kind of girl who would appreciate that sort of thing. I kept thinking of Mary, and it became impossible to sleep. To keep my hands from distraction, I clenched them in prayer.

Make me pure, oh, Lord. Make me strong. Don't give up my seat in heaven.

THREE

THE LONG WALK

The day began, as did every day, with a bell at 6:00 a.m. The student body stumbled into the communal washrooms bleary-eyed and cowlicked. It splashed water in its face, tied its tie, pulled a brush through its hair, and herded downstairs, past the classrooms, the dining halls, and the guesthouse, then through a dark, submarinelike passageway into the dimly lit cavern of the new abbey church. There it knelt and battled with unconsciousness as the monks trickled in.

The monks were in their choir stalls in the apse behind the altar, each in his own cubbyhole on two opposing sides. We called it the Rack. The abbot was always among the first to take his place. He was a misshapened little man with an island of hair in the middle of a mostly bald head, a curved spine that forced him to walk with his waist jutting ahead of his shoulders, and a cross around his neck that was two times too big for his body. Despite his diminutive stature, the other monks shrank in his presence. We liked this.

Sometimes during Mass he'd yawn loudly, and occasionally he'd even snore. This morning, however, he filled the silence with the click of his fingernail clipper, which echoed through the church.

About five minutes prior to Mass one of the priests came off the Rack and passed in front of the abbot, genuflected before the central altar, and disappeared into the confessional at the far end of the church. To receive Communion with the stain of mortal sin on one's soul wasn't done. Venial, or minor sins, were forgiven in a prayer before one received the sacrament; peace with God was made on the spot. But a mortal sin separated man from God and man from the church. Confession was the only remedy. Heady stuff, these mortal sins. Murder, rape, and adultery were all there, but so was jerking off. Thankfully a quick Confession could right any wrong of the previous night. The road to forgiveness wasn't long in terms of natural distance, yet it was a parade past every student, brother, and priest on the hill. It was a considerable journey. One could wait until Sunday Confession to get rid of all the other stuff, but this sin, this mortal sin, had to be snuffed out right there and then.

Michael Ashbury slid off the wooden kneeler and onto the pew, made the sign of the cross, then rose and started the long walk past us. The clap of his shoes reverberated off the tiles and up to the domed ceiling, then ricocheted around the church. He genuflected as he passed the altar and bowed his way into the shadowy recesses of the confessional. From two pews behind me someone whispered, "Looks like Mikey had a date with the Palm Sisters."

I covered my mouth to hold the laughter in, then looked over at Eric kneeling next to me to see if he'd heard it, too. But he was staring straight ahead. Eventually he stood, waited for us to make way, then slipped out. He followed Michael Ashbury and they were forgiven.

Halfway through Mass the frog—silent for a week—decided to join in again. We all turned our attention to the back of the church, and a few people began snickering. Brother Thomas swooped down from the Rack, pulled a swift genuflection in front of the altar, and scurried to the back of the church. Frantically he searched the little fountain and pool. Then he spotted it. He flipped his scapular around his back, tucked it into his belt, rolled up his sleeve, and knelt.

A few seconds later there was a splash and then Brother Thomas straightened with a handful of dripping frog. He took the intruder to the main doors and pushed the handle down. It was locked. He marched to the side entrance and found that door locked, too. We all stared, waiting to see what he'd do next. Red-faced and fuming, Brother Thomas marched the frog past us, bowed abruptly to the altar, then continued out of the back of the church and down the hall in search of an unlocked door to the natural world.

✻

I waited beside our table as everyone else took their places. Even after Mass finally ended, we weren't allowed to speak. I made the mistake of talking before breakfast my very first morning at Saint John the Divine, and my greetings were met with blank stares. Finally one of the seminarians shushed loudly, index finger to lips. It was later explained to me that the Morning Calm was not to be disturbed until Father Gregory, seated alone at the head table, tinkled his little bell.

"What h-happened last n-n-night in the Cave?" Connor asked, reaching his arm past my face for four slices of toast.

"None of your business."

"What's s-s-stuck up your b-butt, William?"

"Nothing. I already told you everything. The Calling, my behaviour, the usual."

Connor slurped his three-sugared coffee and stuck a piece of toast into his mouth. "You seen the p-p-picture yet?"

"What picture?"

"Show him."

Jon slid a Polaroid across the table facedown. Father Gregory glanced up from his mush and morning paper, and Connor subtly moved a napkin over the photo. When Father Gregory looked back down and ruffled his paper, I pulled out the photo and flipped it over. It looked like an out-of-focus finger sticking straight into the air. It was too close to the camera, and the flash had turned it yellow-white. What was in focus and recognizable was Father Gregory's high-backed chair and desk. You could even make out some of the books. It was definitely the Cave—that much was certain. I looked at Connor. "What the hell's this?"

"Tom is the K-King. If you can b-believe that's his d-dink."

The dare had stood unchallenged since last year. Some of the freshmen, now sophomores, had dreamed it up. It involved unauthorized entry into the chamber, an erection, and photographic evidence. I had heard of the dare but was unaware anyone would be stupid enough to attempt it. Studying the photo again, I could tell what it was now. Then I looked over at Tom Wolosovic. He was slouched in his chair, a big, dumb grin smeared across his face. The kid would do just about anything for attention.

"And now we have to call him King for the rest of the year?" I asked Connor.

"Yep. He also made thirty bucks in s-side bets."

"I'm not calling anyone King," Eric said. "Especially for something as disgusting as that."

Jon took another look, then passed the photo to the next table. They passed it back to Tom. Connor eyeballed him and said, "The K-King." Tom smiled big, as if this were the finest moment of his life.

"I don't think I can eat anything now," Eric said.

Father Gregory peered over his paper again and unleashed one of his all-purpose cease-and-desist frowns. We looked down at our plates.

"The food is worse than last year," Jon said, chasing the mush around his bowl with the back of his spoon. "They didn't seem to get the message. Maybe it's time to reorganize SNAC."

SNAC, the Student Nourishment Advocacy Coalition, consisted of eleven disgruntled seminarians: the four of us, three other juniors, a smattering of sophomores, and our newest member, Michael Ashbury. SNAC was concerned about "the quality and quantity of food available at this and similar institutions." Father Gregory had dismissed our complaints, and our parents weren't much more sympathetic. They wouldn't sign the SNAC manifesto. "I couldn't feed you for what they charge for room, board, *and* tuition," my father had exclaimed. "Besides, you're going for free. You'll shut your trap and like it!"

SNAC mostly organized smuggling runs to town or the corner store for supplements: chocolate, potato chips, gum, candy. Recently, however, SNAC had become more political again. Eric had taken it upon himself to write a letter to the B.C. Ministry of Education. He was given a surprisingly polite "Thanks for your concern, but we know what we're doing" reply.

"I'm thinking of sending samples," Eric announced.

"Of what?" I asked.

"I thought you knew. We're sending samples of food for nutritional analysis to the person in charge of school food programs. I've worked out the calories, you know."

People started bringing their cups and plates back to the cart— new kids and keeners eager to be first sitting up straight in class. I got up and filled our empty pot of coffee, then noticed Todd Fowler setting a course for our table.

Todd's uniform didn't fit him properly. Although he had been tall for as long as I could remember, he hadn't gotten around to letting out the hem of his pants or moving up a jacket size or two. It wasn't that he was bulking up or growing a gut; it was only that his hands and legs poked down three or four inches more than normal. I always thought that made him look as if he had just landed after jumping feet first out of an airplane. He once told me that blazers with short arms were all the rage. He even pushed his sleeves a little farther up to exaggerate the effect. I actually saw this in a magazine and was momentarily impressed. It didn't, however, explain Todd's pants.

"This isn't a coffee house," Todd finally said, wiping his nose on the back of his wrist. "Pinch it off."

I suppose in any other school, where there was at least the appearance of democratic institutions, a president was elected through a popularity contest. Not at Saint John the Divine. The upperclassman who had been at the school the longest, in this case Todd, was the Senior Senior. Todd had been doing time at Saint John's since grade nine. So had three other members of the senior class. In a circumstance like that the line of succession became alphabetic. Todd Fowler preceded Tony Morino, Rob Parker, or Francis Tate. Therefore, Todd was Senior Senior. There were only nine seniors at Saint John's that year and they mostly kept to themselves, with this one notable exception.

"W-w-what's your p-problem, Todd?"

The fact that Connor was about half a foot shorter than Todd, and a year younger, didn't matter much. Connor wasn't afraid of anyone.

"Look, I'm just trying to do my job. Can't you guys see you're the last ones in here? These guys've got to clean this place up in the next five minutes." Todd gestured toward Michael Ashbury and another cowering grade niner, one of those little anklebiters I saw nearly every day but whose name I never bothered to remember. You had to earn that. They were holding dishtowels and brooms at the ready. "You guys are holding them up."

As Senior Senior, Todd operated as housemaster and ensured everything was cleaned on time and put in proper order before the first bell rang. Being Senior Senior was his lot in life. Granted, having to make sure washrooms, dorms, hallways, and classrooms were up to scratch wasn't the most sought-after career. Because there was no cleaning staff at Saint John's, we all had a part in the daily upkeep of the place.

Todd turned and stuck his finger in Michael Ashbury's face. "Make sure these guys clean up after themselves, or I'm taking it out on *you*, Ass-berry." He poked him hard in the chest.

Then the unthinkable occurred. Michael took a swing at Todd's finger, but missed. Todd quickly retaliated with a sharp slap across the back of Michael's head. We all jumped out of our chairs in unison, Jon's tumbling backward and crashing on the floor. No one moved. There were no monks, no other witnesses The power structure had crumbled in less than a second.

"He's with us," Jon said. "Leave the kid alone."

Todd glared back with an expression that was supposed to make us think he was barely in control of his superhuman rage. His reign had barely begun and already his bluff had been called. Michael's breathing was fast and audible. I sat down and took a sip of my coffee to signal the end of the standoff. Todd shoved past Michael, then stomped down the hall to spread sunshine someplace else.

✸

The first bell rang loud and long as I sauntered along the hall. Freshmen intensified their scurrying, grabbing forgotten books, checking and rechecking the numbers on classroom doors. I knew all too well where I was going. I also knew that after the first bell there would be five minutes until the second. I decided to spend them all on Mary.

The phone booth in the foyer provided the only real measure of privacy in the entire seminary. The heavy wooden door closed tight. It was quiet in there below the one naked bulb, which illuminated a tiny wooden shelf, a well-used phone book, and a telephone from the Middle Ages—heavy and black with a cloth-covered cord.

"Hello," I said into the receiver. "Is your sister home? Well, isn't she supposed to be going to school in an hour? Okay, I'll wait." The seconds ticked by. Finally I heard Mary slide across the linoleum in her slippers. "I was just about to head to class and I was thinking about you," I said. "I can't wait to see you. Will you be here Sunday? Actually it's 7:58. Anyway, I wanted to tell you that when I'm lying in bed tonight, just before I fall asleep, I'll be thinking about you. If you think about me at the same time, it'll almost be like we're in bed together."

The second bell rang as I approached the classroom door. I turned the handle and bounded in when the ringing stopped. Father Gregory looked up from his notebook, then back down again. "Our first class together and you've already used up your one and only favour. Take your seat, William, then you can tell us your thoughts on transubstantiation."

"Transubstantiation," I said, en route to my desk, "is...a...central tenet of our faith."

"Sit down."

"Turning bread and wine into the body and blood of Christ," I said. "But the appearance of bread and wine remains."

He flipped through his folder and read something, while we sat at our desks writing the date at the top of blank sheets of notebook paper. The entire junior class was there, staring straight ahead, waiting for the start of what should be the easiest course of the semester.

Usually, if you just took part in class discussions and did the homework, religion was a bankable A. The only problem was that Father Gregory hadn't taught a course in over five years. He'd been too busy with administrative duties to teach a class. No one knew what to expect.

We waited and waited. Father Gregory was a great lover of the pregnant pause. Eventually he took a deep breath, then snapped into action. "My apologies for starting this class a week late, but as you know we've all had to make allowances in Brother Stephen's absence."

He grabbed a pile of papers and handed them to Eric, who was sitting in the front row. Eric got up and distributed them around the class, the intoxicating aroma of mimeograph fluid spreading like a billowing cape behind him. When I got my course syllabus, I held it to my nose and inhaled deeply. It was still wet from the machine. I practically inhaled the purple letters right off the page, and I wasn't alone.

"Stop smelling the syllabus," Father Gregory ordered. "You men are juniors now. Act like adults."

The reading list was long and intense. The Council of Trent, Vatican I, and Saint Thomas More were among the highlights. We scanned the coming semester as Father Gregory revelled in our dismay. "Before we discuss the syllabus and the reading list, I want to start off the class with a discussion. I want to talk about Our Blessed Mother."

Pens clicked in a well-conditioned response.

"No need for notes yet. I only want to talk. Tell me, is Our

Blessed Mother the way to heaven?"

That was a heavily loaded question. While we could all see the trap he was setting, Eric was the one to raise his hand.

"No," he announced. "She is not *the* way, but she guides us *along* the way. To her son, Jesus."

Father Gregory pursed his lips. "Then that leads me to another question: Do we worship Mary?"

"No," Jon said. "We're supposed to venerate Mary. We worship God alone." We'd covered this fine distinction last semester. "But let's talk reality here."

Father Gregory pushed some papers aside, tossed the back of his scapular out of the way, and sat on the edge of his desk. "I'm all for reality."

"Reality is that people like the Mexicans and the Polish worship Mary. They don't just ask her to pray for them. They worship the Black Madonna and that other one, Our Lady of Guadeloupe. You can't say people who can't even read know the difference between *venerate* and *worship*."

"Wrong." Eric turned in his seat and confronted the heretic. "Poland and Mexico and Fatima...and Lourdes...and a few other places all have a special relationship with Mary. They know who God is. They know who died on the cross. They're just giving her the honour she deserves—and people in Poland can read!"

Jon shook his head. "They worship those statues. They say some of those things cry and bleed and stuff like that. They get down and crawl on their knees along roads and up mountains to visit a picture. Sounds like worship to me."

"I can't believe you! What's your problem?" Eric shook his head. "These people are only following her to her Son. You sound like a Jehovah's Witness or something."

Father Gregory raised his hand. "Let's keep away from personal attacks, shall we? Stick to the issues."

Connor had had his hand up since the battle had begun. Father Gregory pointed to him. "Who w-w-was the only one to stick by Him w-w-when He was on t-the cross? His disciples skipped out. Mary w-was the only one."

"No, she wasn't," Jon, corrected. "So was Mary's sister, plus Mary Magdalene and that other Mary, the mother of the apostles James Major and John. Besides, what does that have to do with anything?"

I forced my way in. I had no idea why Jon was so agitated, but it seemed as if he needed backup. "What about the fact that we pray the rosary every day? The full rosary is made up of a hundred and fifty Hail Marys and only fifteen Our Fathers. I'm not keeping score, but it seems like she's ahead ten to one."

Eric turned his back on us. "You're sick. You know you're supposed to be thinking about God when you say the rosary."

Jon wouldn't let it go. He was tainted, after all. His dad was born a Lutheran. "Why don't we just pray straight to God? I mean, is she going to tap him on the shoulder and say, 'Give this kid a break as a favour for your mom?' Seems kinda weak to me."

Father Gregory's arms were folded across his chest. He started picking lint off the front of his black scapular. "Jon, you bring up an interesting question, but I think you're being confrontational for effect. However, these are the kinds of issues we'll be discussing this semester. We're going to get to the bottom of a lot of misconceptions and find the truth." He looked out the window and paused. "Essentially we have two pillars of our faith. Anyone?"

Jon and Eric raced to spit out, "Scripture and church teaching."

Father Gregory continued. "Our Christian brothers outside the church have the scriptures, but they've turned their backs on the nearly two thousand years of tradition and dogma. We have those teachings as our inheritance."

"But Father..." Jon threw his pencil onto his desk and folded his arms. "When you pray—I'm not talking about Mass or the rosary—when you pray by yourself, do you just pray to God, or do you cover all your bases and pray to Mary and the saints, too?"

"It's not a game, Jon. Prayer is prayer. Have a look at those books on your reading list and then look into your heart. You'll see the truth."

"You cover your bases."

Father Gregory hesitated, then stood and straightened his habit. "Yes," he sighed, "I most certainly do."

On the way to lunch I saw Father Albert with a tennis bag. He always looked ridiculous strolling through the seminary in his black habit, his big gut, and the bright blue tennis bag, especially since we knew what was really inside.

The monks were against television. In the entire monastery and seminary there were only two TVs. One was kept locked in a closet in the seniors' classroom—to be turned on by a member of the faculty and only for legitimate educational purposes or for sporting events. The other was small, completely illegal, and constantly on the move from one location to the next.

One day the previous year Father Albert had discovered that a freshman named Harold Redinski was harbouring a portable TV in a tennis bag. Quietly he pulled Harold aside and struck a friendly bargain. In return for his silence Father Albert asked to borrow the bag once a week in order to watch his favourite sitcoms. At a prescribed time Harold would leave it sitting by his desk. Father Albert would walk by, pick it up with comic nonchalance, and calmly transport the contraband to the privacy of his cell. He even went out and played tennis once, just to keep up appearances.

When I saw Father Albert shuffling through the hall that day, toting the bag with the tennis racket zipped to the side, whistling the theme to *All in the Family*, I asked him about his game. He smiled, told me his backhand needed work, patted me on the head, and continued on his way.

FOUR

COLLATERAL DAMAGE

I held the shaft in my hand and considered its girth and weight. It was long and sharp and perfectly balanced. It made me feel like a savage. I began to run, then, as if the javelin were eager to fly, it left my hand and sailed through the smoke-grey sky. It punctured the ground fifty yards away, pricking the earth like a giant silver needle.

Jon stood with his hands in his pockets, his javelin stuck in the ground before him. "Brother Ambrose said he'd cook up anything we bring back, as long as we clean it."

"That's because he doesn't think we can catch anything," I said.

I stood back to give him room. Jon plucked his weapon out of the grass, took a few skipping steps, and hurled it into the air. It skewered the field ten feet farther than mine.

Brother Ambrose had hairy fingers and dishpan hands. He was a swarthy little man who always smelled like flour and BO. He wore his cook's white apron and paper chef's hat more than he wore his habit. He ordered the supplies, planned the meals, directed the preparation and cooking of every meal for forty-one monks, 109 seminarians, and anywhere up to two dozen guests. He always kept a supply of cookies hidden in a box by the knives.

Out of the corner of his eye he'd catch the glint of metal doors swinging open and grab a big knife or a meat cleaver in one hand and continue punching dough or cleaning lettuce with the other. When we asked for a cookie, he'd always say we didn't deserve it, but gave us one, anyway. Just one. If we begged for more, or made a move for the cookie box, he'd tap the knife on the counter and say, "C'mon, little man, give it your best shot. I'll cut off your hand and feed it to you."

The cookie was usually excellent—except for those Christmas things he made with the little squares of coloured formaldehyde fruit. Sometimes the cookies he handed over had the flavour of whatever he was working on—gravy-infused chocolate chip or stewed-tomato peanut butter cookies. We'd eat them just the same.

Brother Ambrose had no time for the Student Nutrition Advocacy Coalition. That was made plain from the start. It took him six months to calm down and forgive us SNAC boys for suggesting something was wrong with the food. But he seemed to be over it with the new school year. Plus we had changed our tactics. Now we went over his head directly to the rector. Despite all that, I liked him and wanted to show him I wasn't all bad. I wanted to waltz into his kitchen and present him with a freshly killed grouse or pheasant.

Jon pulled his javelin out of the field and cleaned the mud off the tip with his fingers. "They think we're hunting with slingshots. They'd freak if they knew we'd taken these."

After passing the lower field, we found it difficult to weave through the densely packed trunks with nine-foot aluminum spears. The Douglas firs and hemlocks were thick on Mount Saint John. They held up a dark green canopy some hundred feet above. The forest floor was dim and moist with the sweet mushroom smell of rotting needles and leaves. Only ferns and Oregon grape seemed able to flourish here.

The pheasants were usually up in a field on the east side of the slope. It was occasionally used as a cow pasture but had sat untouched all summer, the tall golden grass reaching wheatlike proportions. When we emerged from the woods at the edge of the clearing, I heard the beating of wings but couldn't see what it was. I hurled my spear into the grass for practice.

We walked around the field a few times and found only a couple of crows. Then, just when we decided to walk across the middle of the field, we saw a big male pheasant. He strutted with his red head cocked and long tail trailing regally behind him, taking careful steps as we readied our spears.

"At the same time," I whispered. Jon nodded, and we crept a few paces closer, within thirty feet. I extended my left arm and drew the weapon back with my right, then whispered, "Ready, set, go!"

Both shots went wide and one clanged loudly against a rock. The bird jumped awkwardly, then ran into the grass. Jon grabbed his spear, reloaded, and fired. Another miss, but much closer this time. When I grabbed my spear, I noticed the tip was split. Brother Fulbert, our coach, would kill me. Jon got off a few more shots, but by that time the bird had made it to the trees and had disappeared into the shadows. I showed the javelin tip to Jon. "Why does this shit always happen to me?"

"Happens to everybody. You just make a bigger deal about it."

"Oh, really? What am I supposed to do now? This thing's worth over a hundred bucks."

"Put it back in the equipment room with the bad tip down and let someone else discover it. Unless you have a hundred bucks, it's your only option. Or you can get the money from your dad."

"I'm not getting anything from my dad."

"Okay." He planted his javelin in the grass and lay down beside it. "Do what you have to."

"First of all," I said, glaring at him, "a hundred bucks is worth something to us because we don't have money lying all over the place. Second, my dad and I aren't talking."

Jon casually crossed his legs at the ankles and propped himself on his elbows. "You know, I'm getting a little sick and tired of your rich guy, poor guy bullshit. I didn't ask to be rich, which I'm not, and you didn't ask to be poor, which you're not. My family does have more money than yours. That's just the way it goes. I don't have a problem with you because of what your dad does or doesn't do, or how much he makes. I don't have a problem. *You* have the problem."

I reached into my pocket for a cigarette and jabbed it between my lips. "I wasn't getting mad at you because you're rich. I was just—"

"Why are you so pissed off at your dad, anyway?"

I lit the cigarette, then shoved my javelin into the ground. "Because he's a creep."

There was rustling in the grass behind us. I crouched down and grabbed a rock. A raven flew out of the grass and landed on a nearby tree. It started squawking, alerting every member of the animal kingdom to our presence. I threw the rock at the bird and hit the tree trunk below the branch it was sitting on. It jumped a bit, then quickly settled back into its nonstop monologue. I bent, grabbed another rock, and hurled it at the bird, striking its breast. It tumbled and flapped as it hit a few branches on the way down, finally landing on the ground in a luminous black heap.

Jon sprang to his feet. "You totally nailed it. Why did you do that?"

We ran to the injured bird and squatted. It shook one wing and dragged the other on the ground. Its frenzy increased as we circled it. The bird stretched its neck repeatedly, then began panting. It was going to die.

"You can't eat these things," Jon said. "Put it out of its misery."

"Maybe we can nurse it back to health and keep it for a pet or something."

Jon looked at me sourly, then grabbed the flopping mess. It was too far gone to resist. He seized its head, stood, and whipped it around in a circle. The flapping stopped. Then he tossed the limp body into the grass, walked over to his javelin, and sat. "You're an asshole."

I found a soft spot in the forest floor, dug a hole with a stick, and gently laid the raven inside. It had a dark beauty like I'd never seen—glossy, almost purple. Like the last seconds of twilight. I filled in the hole, gathered some rocks, and piled them on the mound. Then I sat next to Jon. "I didn't mean to do that."

"I know."

We sat like that for a while, not knowing what to do next.

"Can I tell you something?" I picked a daisy and got up again, pulling the petals off one by one.

"Yeah."

"My dad doesn't want me around. I don't want him around. Me being out here at the Sem is the best thing for both of us. That way I don't have to deal with him and he knows I'll keep quiet."

"About what?"

"About the fact he's cheating on my mom. He's screwing some woman in Montreal and my mom has no idea. I'm the only one who knows."

Jon looked at me thoughtfully. "Isn't he a deacon or something in your parish?"

"Knight of Columbus. He also runs that newsletter for the archdiocese that slams anything he and his friends don't agree with. Some people call it the *Catholic Inquirer*."

I told Jon about how I was sick one day last summer. My brother and sisters were home and we had two cousins staying with us. Everyone else had gone out with my mom to the water slides. I was in my room with the door closed. He must have forgotten I was there. It was too hot to sleep, so to keep my mind off vomiting, I escaped into *The Lord of the Rings*.

My dad called her up from the living room. You could hear everything in that house. He told her how much he missed her and how beautiful she was. How he thought about her all the time and how his body ached for her. I was in total shock. I threw my book against the wall, making a dent in the drywall. He heard it and hung up the phone. That was when my mom and everyone came in. I got up and walked out to where they were standing, all sunburned and happy, loading stuff into the refrigerator. I asked my dad, "Are you off the phone yet?" My voice was cracking. "I can't sleep with you yakking on the phone to your...*friend* all day." And then I started crying.

Jon whistled. "Holy..."

"You should have seen his face. My mom wanted to know why I was crying, and I made up some stupid excuse about puking and feeling sick. Then she looked at my dad and asked if he was feeling okay. The creep."

I turned away from Jon and looked back to where I'd buried the raven. "That night I was on my knees saying rosary after rosary. I wanted God to turn my dad around and I wanted my mom protected from finding out. When my knees gave out, I went to bed and prayed some more. I held my arm straight in the air as long as I could, holding the rosary beads, offering up the pain. Stupid, huh?"

"No."

"Then I made a promise to God."

"What kind of promise?"

I took a deep breath to calm myself. "I've never told anyone this, except a couple of priests. I..." My heart knocked inside my rib cage. "I sometimes have problems with..." Jon had a blank expression. I started again. "Have you ever had problems with...yourself? You know, when you're alone?"

"What do you mean? Chokin' the rope?"

I nodded.

He glanced at the ground and scratched the back of his head. "Yeah, sometimes."

"Well, I promised God I'd give it up forever if He'd just fix things. Make my dad smarten up, make him love my mom again, protect her. Well...I did it again." My bottom lip quivered. "Then my grandpa died. I know it's not my fault he died, but I keep doing it. I can't stop it. I broke a promise to God."

"I do it all the time," Jon said. "During the day, after dinner, in bed. Sometimes I sneak out to the woods. I can't help myself, either. Who can?"

"It's a mortal sin."

"Ah, Bill... Then the whole world's going to hell. Everyone does it. I'm pretty sure. Don't forget that Jesus had one, too. Don't you think He knows how it is? You're not a bad person, and playing with yourself has nothing to do with your grandfather dying. Think about it. When he was young, I'm sure your grandpa did it, too." Jon got up and stood in front of me.

"I know it's stupid, but I had to tell someone and you're the best friend I've got, so you're the lucky bastard." I looked away, and then he reached out and hugged me.

My family wasn't much for hugging. In fact, the only times I could remember my father hugging me were after I broke my hand in grade two and the day my grandfather died. I couldn't remember the last time I hugged my brother, and I certainly hadn't hugged a friend before. Jon clasped me tightly. At first it felt strange, as if we weren't supposed to be doing it. Then I hugged him back and, for a moment, I almost felt free.

FIVE

MARK OF FAITH

Having our loins girded, therefore, with faith and the performance of good works, let us walk in His paths by the guidance of the Gospel, that we may deserve to see Him who has called us to His kingdom.

—The Rule of Saint Benedict

We descended the hill packed tightly into the back of the Volkswagen van. You could cram fifteen seminarians in there with no problem. At the Seminary of Saint John the Divine everyone was compelled to perform a good work on the first and third Sunday of every month. Bingo at the old folks home seemed an easy way to go.

Saint Theresa of Jesus Nursing Home was a converted elementary school on the outskirts of Ennis. The water fountains were low to the ground and the washrooms were still labelled BOYS and GIRLS. The residents needed as much supervision as children, so I thought that was appropriate. They slept in the old classrooms and spent most of their time in the cafeteria, whose walls were covered with pumpkins and witches cut out of orange and black construction paper—courtesy of the grade-three class of the plush new parish school. Halloween was still a month off, but there they were, just the same. At least there weren't any construction-paper tombstones emblazoned with RIP.

"B-6, B-6." Emcee Eric pulled the plastic balls out of the little chute and announced the game. There weren't many luxuries at Saint Teresa's, but somehow the place managed a deluxe air-driven bingo-ball machine.

Most of the residents were in wheelchairs. Some were hunched over, drooling. One old girl was seated with a blanket neatly tucked across her lap. She sat with her back erect as if she were a dancer ready to spring into a pirouette. Perfect posture. The men had five-day beards or hit-and-miss shaves. The place was clean enough, but it had the sweet smell of decay.

We were sprinkled among the general population, helping slide the little red windows over numbers that had been called out, offering conversation. We were there to brighten their lives with our fresh-faced smiles and spice things up with some gambling. God's work. The prize was a bunch of candy, which was a bit of a joke. They always got as much candy as they wanted, anyway. Anything to keep them from acting up.

Mr. Thorpe wasn't a Catholic, but his wife and kids were. He was a railway man who had decided to get a philosophy degree after his wife died and his kids grew up and promptly moved away. Although he was in a wheelchair, you could tell he must have been huge, probably six foot three or better. And he was always clean and well groomed. There was no hair growing out of his ears or on the bridge of his nose. He said he was a freethinker.

"What's that?" I asked.

"Are you a fool?"

"No."

"It isn't Chinese, boy. Freethinker. Someone who unchains his mind. Someone who uses what nature put between his ears. Freethinkers think freely—about everything."

"Then I'm a freethinker, too."

"No, you're not. But there's still hope."

"N-33." Eric took a sip of ginger ale. We got free pop and as many brownies and Rice Krispies squares as we could eat. The nurses were grateful for a break. "N-33."

I always sat next to Mr. Thorpe. No one ever came to visit him, and I thought I could do him some good. Plus he didn't fart or say crazy things like "You stole my feet! You stole my feet!" I'd heard that and worse. Much worse.

Some of the old women swore. And I'm not talking about *shit* and *damn*. They said dirty words in combinations you never thought possible. Prim, proper old ladies—like the one sitting up straight. Usually it came out when someone else called, "Bingo!" The previous year one old lady leaned over and whispered in my ear that she wanted me to screw her. Hard. "With your pecker," she added, in case I didn't know. She must have kept this stuff bottled up her whole life. Sitting next to her wasn't doing any good.

Mr. Thorpe didn't cling to me when I showed up and didn't cry when I left. He acted like a normal but generally pissed-off person. I sat with him three times in a row before he indicated he cared one way or another. I think he liked me. Today he seemed spry. "I'll bet you a buck I can tell you who'll win," he said.

"How do you know?"

"You'll have to pay to find out. Unless you think you know something I don't."

I looked around. The odds were in my favour. "Okay. I'll bet you a buck you can't name the person who'll win the next round. I don't have to choose the right one. I'm just betting you can't."

"Lawyer in the making. Deal."

He wrote down "Mrs. O'Malley" on a slip of paper and handed it to me. She was new. I'd never heard of her before.

"She runs ten cards at once and she cheats," he said.

"How do you cheat at bingo?"

"She'll call 'Bingo,' then pitch a fit when they try to question her. They'll give in to make her pipe down."

"We'll see."

The hum of the bingo-ball machine and Eric's steady monotone were putting a few inmates to sleep. A little later Mr. Thorpe quietly asked to be removed.

"The game isn't over yet," I said. "I still want my buck."

"Now. Please. Just roll me out now."

I had my own card going and I was halfway through a brownie. I was determined to win the game myself. Sighing, I slowly stood.

"C'mon, boy. *Please.*"

I rolled him past the other fogies and toward the door.

"Faster!"

"Calm down."

As soon as the words left my lips, I heard something dripping from the wheelchair and onto the white tile floor. He covered his face. I stopped, glanced down, and saw the puddle of piss trailing behind us. I had walked right through it.

"Mr. Thorpe, I..."

He wouldn't look up. I rolled him toward the nursing station where a black nurse peered at me, then at Mr. Thorpe. She nodded and waved me off. I tried again to apologize. "Mr. Thorpe, I..." He turned and punched my thigh with his tightly clenched fist.

"Little bladder problem," the nurse observed.

Mr. Thorpe shook his head and studied the floor. "I'm so sorry, Gina."

"Don't you worry, sweetheart. We'll get you fixed right up."

I backed away and left him there.

Ten minutes later Mrs. O'Malley called "Bingo!" and then started sobbing when asked to show her card.

Eric didn't ask twice. He raised her hand and proclaimed, "We seem to have a winner!"

✴

I woke up with Eric sitting on my bed, poking my shoulder. He wore pajamas buttoned to the neck and, although he had been in bed for several hours, his hair was still in fine shape.

"Bill," he whispered, "I need you to come with me." His breath

48

was so bad I thought it would singe my eyelashes.

"What? I'm tired. Go back to bed." I rolled over and covered my head.

"Bill, I'm serious. I need you to come with me. I have...a problem. *Please*."

I squinted at him. Finally I pushed him off my bed and sat up. "This better be good."

I glanced up at the dark ceiling for reflected light from Father Gregory's office and listened for the feather-brush sound of his slippers. Satisfied, I got up, pulled on pants and a T-shirt, and followed Eric out of the dorm.

As we padded down the stairs, the only noise was the clicking of the bones in our bare feet. When we finally entered the rec room, I grabbed his shoulder and turned him around. "Okay, Eric, what gives?"

"Not yet. In the piano room."

I followed him through the door beside the little stage and closed it behind us. Originally a stairwell leading to the wings of the rec-room stage, the little space had been enclosed and soundproofed with thick foam tiles. There was barely enough room in there for the upright piano, let alone a student and Father Albert. Eric flicked on his flashlight and sat on the piano stool.

"I'm listening," I said.

He took a deep breath. "I don't know whether to be totally scared or totally happy. I don't even know if I believe it."

"Believe what?"

"Just listen before you say anything, Bill. Don't interrupt."

"*Excuse me*."

"Do you believe in the stigmata?"

"Holes in the hands and feet?"

"And in the side. From the spear a Roman soldier pierced Him with."

"Well, I guess," I said. "There've been cases. Saint Francis for sure."

"You're going to think I'm crazy."

"I already think you're crazy."

"I was praying for a sign," he said, undeterred. "A sign I was on the right path, whether I should become a monk. I was praying for God to give me a sign about what I should do. The next day, *the very next day*, I woke up with this."

He stood, unbuttoned his pajama top, and tossed it on the floor. Then he pulled his T-shirt over his head and presented his right side. He pointed his finger and I followed with the flashlight. And there, just above his hipbone, was a raised lump half an inch wide and four inches long. It glowed red.

"I noticed it when I woke up this morning. It's getting worse. It burns, Bill. It burns real bad and it's all I can do not to touch it."

I sat on the stool and looked up at his anxious face. "Eric, what gives you the idea it's the stigmata? What about your hands and feet? Besides, it doesn't look anything like a spear gash. You must have hurt yourself, then had a nightmare."

"It could *become* a gash. I've been reading. Tons. It happens to people who are chosen." He sighed deeply, and I wondered if he ever brushed his teeth. "I don't know if I believe it, either, but I asked for a sign from God. What am I supposed to think?"

"Look, I'm gonna save you a ton of embarrassment here." Flashing the beam on his skin again, I reached out and touched the sore. It was warm. I pressed it, and Eric whined as if he were in divine pain. "You've got yourself a boil or the mange or something, but I don't think—"

The door swung open and Father Gregory stood before us, staring. He looked at the clothes on the floor, then at me on the stool with the flashlight at Eric's bare belly. No one said anything for a moment. Father Gregory slowly reached down, picked up Eric's T-shirt, and handed it to him. "I'm confident there's an explanation," he said.

Of course, we had to tell him everything. Eric showed Father Gregory the "wound," which was promptly diagnosed as nonstigmatic. The monk said it looked like the symptomatic onset of scabies or some other mite-induced rash. He wanted to know if Eric's "personal physician" concurred. I offered the boil/mange theory, and he thanked me for my considered opinion.

On the way back upstairs Father Gregory said that regardless of potential supernatural phenomena, I would be well advised not to make any more secluded, late-night examinations of my fellow seminarians.

Eric spent the rest of the night quarantined in the infirmary and the next day at the doctor's office in Ennis. Although I didn't whisper a word, news of the false stigmata spread, and Eric became the Laughingstock of the Week. He came back with a patch over his side, a large jar of salve, and photocopies of everything there was to know about hookworm. I went straight to the washroom, scrubbed my hands with carbolic soap, and rinsed with hydrogen peroxide.

SIX

GRACE

One floor down in the sophomores' classroom someone was practising violin. Anklebiters could be heard skipping downstairs to the rec room, and every few minutes Connor's unrestrained, unmistakable laugh sailed up to the window from the fresh mown grass below.

The entire seminary was caught in that peaceful slack tide of evening. That time after dinner and before study hall when we were allowed to manage a precious ninety minutes of freedom. Ordinarily Jon and I would go for a walk, or I'd play my new guitar as he bashed away on the drums. This night, however, would be completely different. I changed out of my uniform and into Jon's brand-new corduroy pants and plush velour shirt.

Jon was stretched out on my bed, his hands clasped behind his head, watching the preparations. "That's more like it."

"Thanks." I combed my hair in the wardrobe mirror. His clothes were always new and in style and they looked much better on him.

I borrowed them only on special occasions.

"So," he asked, "are you in love with her or what?"

"Puh-leez."

"In like?"

"In moderate-to-deep like." I sprayed some of Eric's mousse in my hand and streaked it along the sides of my head. After it was too late, I wondered if the can could transmit worms. "Haven't seen her since last year," I said, surveying the overall effect. "Plus we didn't really spend much time talking."

Jon got up, grabbed a chair, and walked over to the window. He leaned his elbows on the sill and looked out. "Hey, check this out."

I jumped up next to him and glanced down. In the waning summer light I saw Connor and Tom "The King" Wolosovic shooting the breeze on the grass below. Jon directed my gaze over and down half a story to the nursery. In the bay closest to the window was a bare-chested Michael Ashbury, staring into his mirror and flexing his embryonic muscles.

"This is priceless," I said.

Michael Ashbury strained and fawned over himself, making faces at his reflection. Then he left our sight for a moment before coming back with a small stack of books.

Jon leaped down, ran over to his wardrobe, and climbed back onto the chair with his new binoculars. He took a look, shook his head, then passed them over to me. "The kid doesn't have hair one under his arms."

Michael Ashbury was working out with his school books. He had three texts in each hand and was curling them as if they were dumbbells. Between sets of five or six reps, he'd stop and check in the mirror. Then he lay down on his bed and began bench-pressing his homework. But it wasn't heavy enough. The kid disappeared for a second time, then returned with a thick leather-bound Bible. He balanced it on his chest with the other books, then slowly lifted the incredible load.

"You're a stud, Mikey!" I shouted down. "Pump it up, little man!"

Michael Ashbury lost his balance, and the books tumbled to the floor. Rolling off his bed, he quickly pulled on his shirt.

Jon and I jumped off the chair and landed on my bed, laughing our guts out. I went for the binoculars and he wouldn't let go. We wrestled for them.

"Hey, lovebirds," Dean whispered over the partition. "Here comes Father Gregory."

We sprang to our feet, pretending to be busy. Father Gregory paused on his stroll and looked at my messed-up blankets. "We're not using our beds during the day, are we?"

At Saint John the Divine it was considered a minor offence to sit, lounge, or nap on one's bed before rosary. A bed, we were told, wasn't a couch, a chair, or a chaise longue. It was for sleeping. At night.

"Nope," I said, combing my hair again. Jon pretended to be busy as he rummaged through my sports bag where he had hidden the binoculars.

"Then make your bed presentable," Father Gregory said. "Bit by bit we're losing any sense of good order." He sniffed the air. "This place is quickly becoming a flophouse."

☥

As my breathing became deeper, I no longer noticed the varnish fumes. The smell of Mary's scent filled my head. Only a few months earlier this was the abbey church. Now a badminton net was strung across the shiny new floor. Baseball bats and hockey nets were tossed into what used to be the sacristy. The spot where the Communion rail had been was currently a painted free-throw line. Mary and I were upstairs in the storage area, a place made vacant with the removal of the organ pipes. If I let myself think about it, my pulse quickened with guilt. I had to remind myself I was no longer in a church, that now this was merely a gym.

We were on top of a sticky wrestling mat, hidden behind boxes. Mary lay with her head on my chest and her hand under my shirt, gently stroking the new hairs growing below my navel. Her long honey-coloured locks hung straight down only to be encouraged back up by the heat of a curling iron each and every day. Mary's hair was a "feathered" frame for her expectant brown eyes and watermelon-flavoured lip-gloss smile.

Before kissing her I said, "You're the most exciting thing in my life." It sounded like dialogue from a movie, and that was good. Half of the things I had been told about girls turned out to be completely wrong. Well, consider the source—older brother, other kids... Movies were a better teacher. I licked my lips and savoured the sweetness. She made a halfhearted but necessary effort at limiting my advances.

When Mary came to Mass with her parents and brothers on Sundays, it gave me a chance to watch her ass as she strolled past for Communion. She worked hard to avoid looking at me on her way up to the altar, her hands pressed together like the folded wings of a dove.

Two summers earlier, at Okanagan Lake, a girl from a cabin down the beach tried to make a man out of me. The excitement and terror that shot through my body as she worked to pull down my still-damp swimming trunks were more than I could bear. By the time I was free of the wet garment, I had already spent my interest in the situation. I was crushed beyond description. The girl—eight months older and ten years wiser—handled everything tenderly. I wouldn't make the same mistake again.

Kissing the back of Mary's neck where the hairs were soft and fine, I was surprised at how arousing the taste and scent of a neck could be. As I kissed it, she bent her head close to mine and met my eager fondling with an equally passionate rub between my legs. She was a bit rough in an inexperienced sort of way, so it hurt and felt great at the same time. I knew I wasn't much better with what I was doing, so I didn't say anything. It wasn't long before things began churning out of control.

The sound of the key in the door downstairs was unmistakable. Our hands ceased their caressing as the lights came on. We stared at each other and felt our hearts pump hot adrenaline. Mary looked down at her arm, which was buried deep in Jon's new corduroys. Swiftly she pulled it away, and the waistband of my briefs snapped against my belly.

Footsteps came our way. Mary silently encouraged her blouse and open bra into a more presentable position as I worked away at my belt and untucked shirt. The footsteps continued straight for us. We sat up, unable to hide. As the intruder rose to our level, a close-cropped, Velcro-covered head and gangly torso were silhouetted in the light from behind.

"MacAvoy, what the hell do you think you're doin'?" Todd stared down at us, hands on hips.

"If you don't know by now, you better have a chat with your old man."

Mary elbowed me in the ribs.

"I don't have to tell you how many rules you're breaking right now," he said. "So I won't."

"I have five bucks," I said, reaching for my wallet. "Take it. It's yours."

"Do I hear twenty?"

The downstairs door opened and closed again. Mary looked at me, then covered her face with her hands. "What now?"

"Who's in there?" It was Brother Thomas.

No one answered. Todd considered whether to come down to meet him and explain he was in the process of catching us, or remain silent and hope Brother Thomas would close the door and leave. That was a lot for Todd to think about at once. Brother Thomas ascended the stairs.

"They were in here with the lights out," Todd said. "I came to make sure it was locked and I heard them."

"Fine, Todd," Brother Thomas said. "It's almost time for rosary. Why don't you run along?"

Todd left.

"Do you know what time it is?" Brother Thomas asked.

"Around 8:30, I think," I said.

"Smart. Is that Mary O'Brien up there with you?"

"Yes, Brother," she moaned.

"Do your parents know where you are?"

"Uh, I don't *think* so."

"How did you get up here?"

"I walked from town."

"I suggest you go out and wait by the van and I'll give you a ride home."

"No, Brother," she said. "Really, I could—"

"Don't argue with me, young lady. Do as you're told."

Mary stood, straightened herself out, and walked away. As she passed Brother Thomas at the top of the stairs, she looked over her shoulder and smiled back at me.

"William, we can't tolerate this sort of thing," he said. "You know that."

"Yes, Brother."

I was told I was "skating on thin ice" and that I'd "crossed the line" for the last time and that when I broke the rules, the rules would break me, and a host of other time-tested parochial school clichés. When he felt I had enough, he looked at me with what might have been an understanding gaze, but it quickly evaporated.

Outside I walked past the vw van and saw Mary waving from the passenger window. She blew me a kiss across the dim parking lot. I grabbed it in midair and tucked it deep down the front of my briefs.

✹

After an hour of praying for deliverance from temptation, I got out of bed and pulled on track pants in the dark. The only sound was someone flushing a urinal downstairs. I walked out of the dorm barefoot, past Jon and Connor. Dean was sleeping with his mouth wide open, one arm dangling out of bed. As I walked downstairs to the phone booth, I looked up at the clock: it was only 11:10 p.m. I dialled Mary's number with the door open, so I could see, then closed it without turning on the light, sealing myself in absolute darkness.

Mary answered the phone on the first ring and warmly whispered, "Hello."

"I have to tell you something. I want you to know I'll never cheat on you. I swear it. You're the only girl. I'd never do anything to hurt you."

There was a long silence as we listened to each other's breathing. "I know," she said finally. Then I "heard" her smile: the little sound of the corners of her mouth rising, showing her teeth. I heard her brush the hair away from her face. It gently whisked across the mouthpiece of the receiver. "See you Sunday."

"See you in my dreams," I said.

✳

A note was on the table next to my napkin when I came in for breakfast. The entire Saturday that lay so open and inviting suddenly slammed shut in an instant. I read the note again for any loopholes or ambiguities. There were none. "Shit," I said, passing the note to Jon and finishing my mush.

As I marched across the field toward the Bog and cemetery, I saw Brother Thomas trying to make a holly bush into something rectangular. He was using hedge clippers, and it was working. Brother Thomas was out of his black habit and into army-green pants and a tan jacket, the monks' standard-issue casual attire. It was too warm for a jacket, but I knew it would have to be at least 150° before he would take it off. The monks were freaky that way. As I approached him, I took the folded note out of my pocket and held it in my hand.

"Good morning, William." Brother Thomas continued clipping away.

"Morning, Brother. You wanted to talk to me?"

"More to the point," he said, turning and removing his gloves, "I want your help for a little while." Brother Thomas tossed a pair of gloves to me, then gestured at the pile of holly branches and the half-filled tractor wagon. "Written anything lately?" he asked as I started loading up the branches.

"We're on grammar right now. We're supposed to be doing some writing next semester."

"Haven't you written anything on your own?"

"Not since the summer."

"Hmm." Then, after a few minutes of working in silence, he said, "She's pretty."

"Yeah," I said proudly.

He continued chopping at the next holly bush. There were ten of them in a row that would eventually serve as a border between the sloping field and the monks' cemetery. "But is she smart?" he asked.

"Sure. I mean, I guess she is."

He amputated a few more branches. "I was engaged once, you know. Long before I came here, of course. It didn't work out."

I couldn't believe he was telling me this. Usually the monks wouldn't even reveal their real names, the ones their parents gave them, for fear of being taunted by the underclassmen. And here was Brother Thomas telling me he had been *engaged*. It almost meant he was human. Still, I figured it was a brilliant attempt to get me to let my guard down, to like him.

"Is that right?"

"Yes, William, that's right. She was kind and she was beautiful. Probably still is." We worked in silence again. Despite the gloves, I was cutting my forearms on the sharp leaves. It was beginning to look as if I had lost a fight with a cat. "Well, since you're so curious," he finally said, "I'll tell you why it didn't work out."

I kept on loading.

"We met at a dance. She was my sister's friend. We went out for almost a year, then I got impatient. I kept at her for months, even though she wanted to wait until we were married. I finally wore her down. And then that was the end of it. She didn't want to see me again."

I felt uncomfortable having him say these personal things. He wasn't supposed to tell me this stuff and I didn't want to know it. "Where's she now?" I asked.

"I'm not sure. I've been told she's married with kids, though."

"Oh."

"I'm not telling you this to convince you to wait until after marriage. If you don't know right from wrong by now, we're not going to be able to tell you differently. I'm only trying to say I've been there and I made a mistake I lived to regret. It wasn't worth it."

He stopped, thought for a moment, then set the clippers down and grabbed a thermos from the tailgate of the wagon. He walked over to me and put his hand on my shoulder, directing me around the hedge to the cemetery. "Let's take a break."

Brother Thomas sat on the grass. As he unscrewed the thermos and poured coffee into the plastic cup, I glanced at the seven tombstones in the corner of the plot and the large, conspicuous empty space. This patch of grass was waiting to absorb the monks as one by one they left life on the surface of the hill. It gave me the creeps, but Brother Thomas didn't seem to mind. He handed me the cup and poured some for himself into the chrome thermos cap.

"Sit down," he said. "Stop hovering."

I sat.

"You know, Saint Benedict had a little job he'd assign men like you—stop me if this sounds like a homily."

"Stop."

He smiled, then continued. "New recruits into the community who valued their individualism and pride more than the community were handed shovels. Then Saint Benedict asked them to dig holes. They asked why, of course, and he simply said, 'Because I ask it of you.'"

I drank the coffee and tried to link this monologue to anything that had been said earlier about women. I couldn't.

"The young novices dug the holes, thinking it must somehow add to the greater glory of God, then they returned to Saint Benedict and said, 'There, we dug the holes as you asked.' Saint Benedict replied, 'Good, now go and fill them back in.'"

"Sounds pretty dumb if you ask me."

"That's precisely what the young novices said. They complained that it made no sense, was a waste of time and labour, and was otherwise totally senseless." Brother Thomas turned and looked directly at me. "Like not being able to wear jeans, for instance."

At Saint John the Divine we weren't allowed to wear blue jeans, rock-star T-shirts, or shirts with logos or slogans of any kind. That, of course, wiped out the wardrobe of most North American teenage boys. When we weren't in uniform, we had to wear collared shirts, cords, rugby pants, or dress pants.

"He was teaching obedience," Brother Thomas said. "Obedience isn't weakness, William. It takes real strength. It's one of the hardest lessons to learn, especially for an intelligent, ambitious young man like yourself." He looked away. "Especially in this day and age."

"I think freedom is more important. No offence, Brother, but I'm not cut out for a life of digging holes and filling them back up again."

"I wouldn't dream of suggesting it. But you do have certain obligations in the here and now. You have a lot to learn before you're ready for the *responsibilities* of freedom."

I was getting bored. I licked my finger and began rubbing the little red holly scratches on my arms.

"Consider this a friendly warning, William."

"Okay, okay. Can I go now? The guys are going to town and I—"

"Don't bring her up here again. I'm not going to repeat myself." He got up to return to work.

"I have a question. You're not the rector. You're not even my English teacher this semester. Why—"

"Let's just say you're my 'special project' this year."

I took a few steps, then stopped. "Did you become a monk because your fiancée dumped you?"

He was annoyed at being asked. His frown gave him away. "No. But don't worry. If Mary cuts you loose, I don't think you're in any danger."

SEVEN

RETREAT

Father Ezekiel was an old, exotic bird. Draped in his chasuble and flanked by his fellow monks, he still couldn't hide it. As he carried the monstrance, with its gilt rays of glory beaming out from the holy centre, his head bobbed like a guinea fowl's. His skull was small and his neck was long and skinny. I was beyond laughing at him. I knelt in awe at how anyone could function with such a debilitating condition.

As Father Ezekiel approached the altar steps, the chant reached a crescendo. To avoid touching the monstrance with his bare hands, he used special stole to carry it to the altar. Inside the little glass case in the middle was the Holy Eucharist, a big white wafer that had become the body of Christ. Father Ezekiel set it down and lit the little coals in the ball-shaped thurible that Tom Wolosovic held suspended from a chain. We sang as they slowly circled the altar, swinging a cloud of incense with the measured *clank, clank* of the thurible against its chain.

"Blessed be God. Blessed be His holy name. Blessed be Jesus Christ, true God and true man. Blessed be the name of Jesus..."

Benediction marked the end of the fall retreat. There were two retreats each year consisting of a weekend of even more intense prayer and spiritual direction. Usually a guest speaker delivered a couple of exhaustive monologues about God, faith, and the world. We learned we were to be *in* the world but not *of* it. During retreats, studying, sports, games, and music—except chanting—weren't allowed; food was cut way back, since we were supposed to be fasting; and no talking was allowed.

After reciting the Divine Praises and meditating in front of the Blessed Sacrament, we filed out of the church and back into the silent seminary. Because tomorrow was a school day we were to read, pray some more, and hit the sack early. Jon and I decided to climb the bell tower instead.

❦

The bell-tower platform was open on all four sides. A complicated gaggle of antennae was suspended high over our heads and, above that, was the underside of a soaring concrete cloister vault. Outside and on top of the tower was a cross that did double duty as a lightning rod. From this small concrete perch the lights of Ennis Valley could be seen winking in the distant haze. Hail Mary Corner, the sharpest turn on the road to civilization, was dark and gloomy. On the other side, the upper soccer field, the tennis court, and the football field were laid out before us. From this vantage point the Bog looked even more squarely contrived.

A couple of years before we arrived on the scene the abbot declared the bell tower off-limits after a seminarian dropped a penny over the railing and hit an old lady on the shoulder. The kid had read somewhere that it was possible to kill people with spare change from the top of the Empire State Building and thought he'd give it a try. The old girl was only spooked, but the abbot was unamused. The bell tower had remained closed to the student body ever since. The front door was always locked, but by climbing onto the roof of the library and squeezing into one of the light shafts near the spiral staircase, Jon and I had discovered we could make our way to the top.

The setting sun left the sky a dark inky blue. As the first stars flickered to life, the temperature began to fall. I leaned over the bell-tower railing and spat. The little white bomb sailed straight down until a breath of wind pushed it into the concrete wall twenty feet above the bushes.

"You're sick," Jon said.

I noticed Jon's new watch as he clung to the railing. It was one of those digital types boasting an LED chronometer with red numerals that appeared when a button was pushed. "Nice watch," I said.

"Like it? It's yours." He took it off and handed it to me.

"What? Didn't your dad give it to you?"

"Forget it. I have another one."

"Not a digital one," I said, handing it back. "I can't take it. It's expensive."

"No, it's not. I'm giving it to you. I want you to have it." Jon grabbed my hand, pressed the watch into it, and pushed it toward my chest.

"I almost forgot," I said, strapping on the watch. "You're loaded. Suddenly I don't feel so bad."

"You're welcome, I think."

Feeling a little embarrassed at this display of generosity, I put my arm around his shoulder. "Thank Daddy Warbucks for me. Keep me in mind when you move up to Rolexes."

Although we had stuffed our beds with seminarian-shaped piles of pillows and clothes, we were banking that Father Gregory wouldn't patrol the dormitories at the close of the fall retreat. Calorie-deprived and lulled into submission, the rest of the student body would shuffle off to bed like good little zombies, wondering why they ever wanted to speak to one another in the first place.

We had brought two wool blankets and a couple of chocolate bars for this expedition. After the sugar rush started to fade, we settled down on the hard concrete floor and listened to the wind whistle through the bells below. Attached to the bells were long ropes that dangled down to a tiny room where three monks pulled and the Angelus rang out each morning, noon, and night. It was a sound that was comforting and confining. The Angelus let you know you had somewhere to be, something to be part of. But it also reminded you your time—your life—wasn't your own. There was a divine order to conform to, a schedule that had existed for centuries and that would continue long after everyone's dust was scattered in the breeze.

Jon and I talked for a while, happy to get out of our heads, to connect again. Then I got drowsy. He wanted to know what I thought about the topic of this year's retreat: the Mystery of the Holy Trinity.

"I don't know," I said. "It's confusing. I'm not sure why God needs three forms—Father, Son, Holy Spirit. I don't know why we just can't say God."

I kept trying to find a comfortable spot. Jon rolled up his jacket and made a pillow, then wrapped himself in his blanket. We hadn't brought any foam pads, so the warmth of our bodies leached into the cold concrete floor.

Jon went on for a while talking about the Trinity, the "Threeness and Oneness." It didn't sound as if he was convinced, though. More important, he said it didn't really matter. We couldn't hope to understand God, anyway. In the end everyone had to follow his own conscience.

"Even Saint John the Divine admitted it," Jon said. "'Love one another, that is the Lord's commandment. And if you keep it, that is by itself enough.' I memorized that one. It helps keep me real."

I was listening to him, sort of, as I yawned. Just to let him know I wasn't being rude, I threw him a bone now and then with "Uh-huh" or "Yeah" or "I can see your point." Then, when I stopped responding altogether, he asked if I believed in angels.

"Don't see why not. They're all over the Bible."

He was silent for a moment. "I've seen one."

I blinked, trying to pull myself awake.

"I saw one in my room three years ago. Before I came here. He was standing near my bed when I woke up in the middle of the night. I wasn't even scared."

I rolled over and looked at him, but it was too dark to see his face clearly.

"I've never told anyone that before," he said.

"You think it was real? How do you know it was an angel and not the Devil?"

"He looked just like us. A little older. About twenty, I think. But I'm sure he was an angel. He didn't have wings or anything like that. He was...beautiful."

"*Beautiful?* What did he say?"

"He didn't say anything. He didn't even open his mouth. All he did was smile, but I understood. He wanted me to know everything was going to be all right and that he was watching out for me. That's when I decided to come to the Sem."

I didn't doubt Jon's story for a second. Perhaps I doubted his interpretation of events, but not his intent. He said he didn't think he was dreaming and that it was my job to believe him.

"It's a little scary," I said.

"Do you believe me?"

"Of course."

"Pray for me. Pray I won't go crazy."

"You're not crazy. You're the most normal person I know. I mean, not normal as in *boring*, but—"

"You're the only one who knows."

We stopped talking as the wind kicked up and the night settled in. The antennae creaked and a train rumbled on the far side of the valley. I said a prayer for Jon, asking God to protect him.

I tried to fall asleep but couldn't get comfortable. That initial flood of drowsiness was now replaced with a fear of being up so high in the dark. I couldn't stop thinking about Jon's story, and the fact that sometimes Satan took on forms that seemed good and pure. Satan, or Lucifer, was once an angel, the best angel. They say he loved God too much. He even tricked some of the other angels into following him. How in hell could Jon tell the difference? I woke him up to ask him.

He rubbed his eyes. "I'm sure it wasn't Satan."

"I don't want you getting tricked."

"Don't worry about me."

"I've never had a friend like you before. It feels like we're…the same."

"Yeah, it's weird. I know what you mean."

A bat flew low overhead, passing through the bell tower without making a sound. We ducked and waited for it to happen again. When it didn't, Jon said he was freezing his balls off and wanted to know if I felt like going back inside.

"No," I said. "Unless you do."

"Then come closer so we can both stay warm."

I moved next to him, and we rearranged the blankets so we had one above and one below. I could smell the chocolate on his breath and the sweat of his armpits, but it didn't bother me. When I turned my back to him, he pressed against me.

Jon twitched and then dived headfirst into his dreams. I could feel the steady rise and fall of his chest. After a few Hail Marys, I drifted off behind him. The last thing I remembered was feeling warm and important.

EIGHT

OFFSIDES

Brother Fulbert, our earnest but somewhat deflated soccer coach, gave the new leather ball to the referee as if he were handing over the baby Jesus. The referee nodded awkwardly, turned, and marched from the sideline to the centre of the field.

Connor stood with his hands on his hips and his eyes on the ball. He swayed back and forth on powerful legs, bent slightly at the knees, ready to spring into action. Eric stood next to him, sizing up the opposing team of Baptists, hugging himself as if there was a chill. Jon was on right wing, temporarily more interested in a clump of grass wedged between his cleats than the outcome of the coin toss. I took deep gulps of air, super-oxygenating my blood for a faster start.

Bobby, Francis, and Dale were halfbacks; Patrick, Dean, and Paul held the fullback territory; Helmut defended the goal. The reduced ranks of Saint John's varsity soccer team stood staring over the precipice of another season. Because the seniors were away in Vancouver for the provincial debate semifinals, the junior men were left to carry the torch alone.

Our opponents won the toss. The kickoff was done, and the Baptist front line spread out for its first assault.

The Calvary Cougars had a considerable edge. They were the most formidable religious school on Vancouver Island. Most were seniors and most were seventeen. They were chosen from the cream of a crop of more than a hundred men. We, on the other hand, were it. Every member of the junior class was on the team. The four guys who weren't on the field in their positions were on the bench in uniform, waiting to spell us when exhaustion or injury occurred. Although we had a shallow gene pool of talent to choose from, we made up the difference in spirit. The urge to "kick Baptist butt" on our own turf was a powerful instinct. In order to defeat the infidels we would pull together so tightly it would be difficult to tell us apart. At least that was the plan. Finally we got the ball.

"Eric!" I yelled. *"Pass!"*

He had trouble getting around their halfback, but when he did he chewed up the real estate between him and the goal with admirable speed. We fell into our triangular assault formation. I ran almost parallel to Eric as he charged up the field, a flurry of elbows, ankles, and knees. Connor hung back ten yards to catch a back pass and to keep from going offside, which he did with reliable consistency. At last Eric relented and passed the ball back to Connor.

Connor wasn't the least bit awkward or clumsy. Although he didn't have Eric's height, his muscular build and the mad look in his eyes were enough to intimidate most opponents. Connor easily deked around the first halfback who made a break for him. He took the ball and shifted into high gear, weaving the prize between all who would oppose him as he made a break for the goal.

Connor, however, still wasn't in the open for the shot. I was on right wing in perfect position, waiting for the pass to come. When we scrimmaged, or played against the Indian kids from the nearby reserve, we'd pass freely, making the assault on the net together as a unit. Today, for some reason, Connor didn't even glance in my direction.

"Connor! I'm open. "Pass the friggin' ball!"

Wanting to be the hero, he took a bad shot on goal—straight into the goalie's arms. Michael Ashbury could have stopped it.

We played on like that into the remains of the first half. They scored twice. Eric, when he saw a chance, would break away down the field and hit whoever was open. Jon and I would try to get a play going, but something was up with Connor. He was running his own show.

After the Baptists nearly scored a third goal, Connor intercepted a pass and bolted straight into a wall of defencemen. He ran around with five Baptists charging him and slide-tackling into his ankles. But he still wouldn't pass the ball. I yelled at him, but he pretended not to hear. They finally took the ball away. It was an embarrassing display of self-importance.

I marched over and shoved him. "What the *fuck* is your problem?"

"Screw you, M-M-MacAvoy."

"I'm serious, man. This is a fuckin' *team* for Christ's sake."

"You Catholics cuss too much," one of the Baptists' halfbacks observed. He had close-cropped orange hair and a thick neck and had been in my way the entire game. "Don't take the Lord's name in vain," he said. "And don't hack my shins."

"Fuck you!" I retorted. Then I turned and started in again on Connor. "Pass the ball for a change."

"Don't be so j-j-jealous. Like I h-h-haven't been trying—"

"Jealous?"

"You haven't s-scored all y-y-year."

Our Baptist friend loved this. A big smile broke out across his freckly face, then he covered his mouth as if he could barely keep the laughter in. "Huh-huh-how about you la-la-ladies getting buh-buh-back to the guh-guh-game?"

Lunging at him, I knocked him over and swung at his head. I connected a few times, but within seconds three of their guys were all over me, trying to ring my neck and get a clean punch in. Connor and Eric joined the fray, but not before my opponent scored a solid, air-evacuating shot at my stomach.

The referee frantically tooted his whistle as Brother Fulbert and the Baptist coach marched in from opposing sides. When we were all pulled apart—muddy, panting and, in the case of ol' Carrot Top, bleeding from the nose—I saw Jon standing near the sideline, well out of harm's way. I felt something sink inside.

Brother Fulbert whacked me across the head with an open hand.

"Ow! For Christ's sake!"

"Watch your mouth!" He came back with another cuff to the cranium and then he hit Connor.

The Baptist coach was about twenty-three years old and looked like a cop. Brother Fulbert was old enough to be his grandfather. The Baptist peered straight into the monk's wise old eyes. "These don't sound like Christian boys to me."

Everyone turned their attention to my bleeding Baptist friend. His head was tilted back, nose pinched. It wasn't all that bad. There was very little blood.

Brother Fulbert pointed at Connor and me. "You two are out of the game. Hit the showers."

That, of course, meant the end of any hope we had of winning. Nick, the anemic math scholar, and marginal Owen were called from the bench to fill our places.

"I'll see you two after the game," Brother Fulbert said, lips tight.

We stomped back up the slope, but the adrenaline was slow to subside. I felt like hitting someone else. Connor put his arm around my shoulder and smiled. I pushed him away. He started to laugh and came back at me again, grabbing my neck and putting me in a head-lock, laughing harder and harder at my escape attempts. I fought with everything I had to get away. Then, no longer travelling forward, we pulled each other down on the grass. After that it got serious.

I started punching him in the thigh, the gut, the groin—anywhere I could reach. I was aiming to maim. He squeezed tighter, and I could feel myself choking.

"Get into those showers *now!*" Brother Fulbert yelled. "Or by God I'll..."

Looking up, we saw every face on the field staring back as Brother Fulbert ran toward us, fist raised high over his head. We both let go, then tore inside as fast as we could.

✳

After rosary we all returned to the classroom to study. Several days of homework had piled up, and the reprieve granted on account of our afternoon showdown with the Baptists was now past. The other seminarians shuffled by on their way from the chapel as I slumped over my desk, trying to keep the pressure off my still-stinging ass. Connor sat across from me, flipping through an old issue of *Sports Illustrated*. He didn't look the least bit bothered.

Word of the "attack" on the Baptists had worked its way up the chain of command before we finished showering. After Brother Fulbert directed the cleansing of our mouths with gritty powdered soap, we were summoned to the Cave. There, Father Gregory told us to grab our ankles so Justice—the nickname of his wide leather strap—could be applied to our backsides. We each got it six times. Neither of us made a sound. Although it still hurt, I could tell Father Gregory wasn't as strong as he used to be.

Eric opened the lid of his desk, revealing his personal shrine. On the underside of the lid he had a big colour picture of Our Lady of Guadeloupe, surrounded by a pantheon of saints. Eric reached past the gaze of the heavenly host and took out his tin of Copenhagen. He closed the desk and put a generous wad of tobacco between his lip and gums. He offered the can to Jon, whom he knew would refuse, then brushed his hands on his pants and slipped the tin into his pocket.

Suddenly, like dogs to a distant whistle, everyone froze and pricked up their ears. Father Gregory's shoes squeaked our way from down at the far end of the hall. I could never forget that sound: a cross between a cricket's chirp and the squeal of a wood screw being tightened. Eric leaped up to join Jon at the window, turning his tobacco-lumped cheek away from the opening door.

Father Gregory strode in and frowned impatiently at Connor and me, waiting for us to look up and officially acknowledge his presence. Eventually Connor closed his magazine and slipped it into his desk.

"I've also decided that your labour will be required down at the barn for the next three Saturdays in a row," he said. "You've embarrassed yourselves, your families, your seminary, and your church. The next time, and there better not be a next time, you'll be sent home for good." Then, addressing the room, he asked, "What kind of animals are we raising here?"

None of us knew.

"If I remember correctly, you have a religion essay due on Friday." He paced between the desks. "And let me remind you—there's no such thing as a Bell Curve in this school. An F is an F just as it was in the good old days. I suggest you get to work."

As soon as Father Gregory closed the door behind him, Eric leaned out the window and let a long string of brown saliva squirt from between his front teeth and into the bushes below. Eric always maintained he was doing his part to keep the world green by chewing tobacco. High-grade fertilizer, he said. I was glad he chewed. Seeing holy Eric with a plug of chaw in his lower lip somehow brought him back to reality. "Time me," he said, moving away from the window.

Eric had many talents, but the one he was most proud of, the one there was absolutely no disputing, was his prowess with a Rubik's cube. For mere mortals the Rubik's cube was designed to test skill at scrambling, then unscrambling the coloured squares on a cube. It was the craze of the day. Eric, however, took things to a much higher level. He lifted the top of his desk and reached in for his logbook and cube. We gathered around to watch. He flipped open his logbook and wrote the date near the bottom. There must have been nearly a hundred entries in there.

Eric threw the cube to Connor, who scrambled it as well as he could and then set it in the middle of Eric's desk. Everyone got quiet as Eric handed his stopwatch to Jon, who held it at the end of an outstretched arm and said, "Ready, set, go!"

Seeing him like that reminded me of The Who's "Pinball Wizard." His elbows were tight to his sides, his hands a blur in front of him. The cube shifted so fast it was difficult to distinguish the colours. Everything was a flickering mass of red, yellow, and blue—like fire.

"Don't you guys ever study?" It was the voice of Dean.

All fifteen members of the junior class were in the room, most of them studying. I hardly noticed any of them, ever. They were colourless and quiet, dreary and dead. They weren't a part of our group and could never hope to be. It surprised me sometimes just how invisible they had become. Dean was looking up from his essay, his forehead resting in his hand. I was the only one to glance up in response to his question. And, without so much as a blink of acknowledgement, I returned my attention to the flame in Eric's hands. The master slammed the cube down on the desk with a flourish.

"Fifty-seven seconds," Jon said. "You're rusty."

Eric was wearing the little coloured stickers off from overuse. The master had two more cubes, but this was his favourite. He had lubricated its guts with olive oil and had risen to such a dizzying height in Rubik's cube ability that no one could hope to touch him. Eric was—in its simplest, purest form—"the best."

"Can't wait to see the times in the nationals this year," he said calmly. "Who wants to bet I'm within fifteen seconds?"

"Come on," Dean moaned, "some of us have a future."

"Unclench, Dean," I said. "You'll give yourself an ulcer and die before all that brown-nosing has a chance to pay off."

The squeak of Father Gregory's shoes approached once more. Eric slipped the cube and log back into his shrine, we scrambled for our seats, and Dean lifted his head to flash a satisfied smirk.

*

Father Gregory had to know we would discuss our grades the moment class was over, but he went through the pretence of privacy just the same. Walking through the class, he handed out our essays quickly, facedown, with the letter grade hidden at the end of the back page. I looked at mine: "The Case for Married Priests." B+.

"Essentially you all performed well," Father Gregory said. "A few flashes of insight, a few lapses of reason. Do you want to discuss your papers now, or shall we leave it for later?"

We were all still reading the red marks, the margin notes, and the lengthy deliberations above the grades. Father Gregory's handwriting was controlled and expressive, masculine and graceful—the way I imagined William Shakespeare had written. In his notes to me he not only thought I had a case, but gave me other sources to support my thesis. Just when you thought you were getting to know somebody...

Another slip of paper was in circulation. I unfolded it under my desk to avoid attracting attention. It was a note in the stunted hand of Connor Atkins. Its message: "REDRO Word of the Day— Essentially."

We all had a few pet words and phrases, favourite figures of speech. Father Gregory had a warehouse full. Connor made a hobby of collecting them in a section of his notebook entitled "The Quotations of Chairman Greg." Anything that was said more than three times per class made the list. Connor sprinkled them liberally throughout his essays.

Our goal was to disrupt order in the most cunning way possible. We were to work the Word of the Day into all of our conversations during class, no matter how insignificant. A score was kept. Anyone who slipped up or didn't include the word in his speech owed a chocolate bar to everyone else who took part.

"Two essays and one exam are behind us, gentlemen," Father Gregory said. "Essentially that leaves two more opportunities to enhance your final grade."

We all looked down to stifle our smiles.

"William wrote a convincing argument for the readmission of married priests into the clergy. Any comments on the subject?"

Jon raised his hand. "There's a worldwide shortage of priests. Essentially, if we allow married priests back in, we increase the number of priests by four hundred percent, or something like that."

"William?"

My task was a little harder. Each mention of the word took you closer to getting caught. "He's right, essentially. But there would also be a cost for allowing them in. They'd have wives and families. You can't ask *them* to take a vow of poverty. Essentially you'd have to pay priests a heck of a lot more than they're getting now."

Double-word score. I was feeling good.

Eric wasn't impressed. "Might as well be Anglican. Anglicans are essentially Catholics who can marry. And they don't follow the pope. Perfect for you, MacAvoy."

Connor wanted in. "And don't f-forget the P-Presbyterians and L-Lutherans. They can m-marry. So can the B-Baptists and M-M-Methodists and b-basically...*es-ssentially* everyone but us."

That was close.

Father Gregory gazed out the window. "Eric had an interesting paper. Ambitious. Tell the class, Eric."

"Well, it has to do with the Vatican and the church's money. I made the case that we should liquidate all church assets and real estate, sell all that stuff in Rome and give it to the poor. We're talking trillions. If Jesus came back today, He would do it in a second. I'm not saying we don't need a pope and an overall headquarters. I'm just saying we could do a lot more with that money if they relocated to a cheaper spot, toned down, and distributed the rest to the missions." He knew he had forgotten something. "Essentially...we're not getting a good enough return on God's money."

Eric was out of body with this one. For the first time in his life he was forming his own opinion on a subject. I was impressed and thought I'd tell him so. "Essentially you've become a freethinker."

Eric turned around. "What's that?" Then, realizing his mistake, he added, "Essentially."

"All right, children, that's enough." Father Gregory took off his glasses and spun around, then wrote the offending word on the chalkboard in big sprawling capitals: ESSENTIALLY. "Just when I think I'm having a rational discussion with young men, I'm reminded that I'm really baby-sitting toddlers. It's beyond frustrating."

Eric owed three chocolate bars. It could have been worse.

Father Gregory looked outside during his pause, the electric hum of the clock above his head the only sound. He walked back to the chalkboard. Just below ESSENTIALLY he wrote FREETHINKER.

"Eric, do you know what a freethinker is?"

"It sounds like someone who thinks without...any restrictions?

He's free to think what he wants?"

"William?"

"He's right, *basically*. Someone who doesn't close his mind, I guess."

Father Gregory put his glasses back on his beak. "A freethinker is someone who rejects dogma, someone who forms his opinions without regard for custom, convention, authority, or the existence of God. Is that you, Eric?"

"I...think freely." Eric's voice was breaking. "I don't stop my mind just because I'm Catholic. I believe in the church, but I don't swallow everything until I've thought about it first."

"Some things must be taken on faith," Father Gregory said. "We can't pick and choose what we like and don't like about following Christ."

Eric was visibly shaken. For once he wasn't armed with a ready answer. "But I have to be free to think about things, don't I?"

"We're entering the realm of semantics," Father Gregory insisted.

Something pulled free of its moorings inside Eric's well-moussed head. "Can't you be a freethinker and a Catholic at the same time?"

Father Gregory sighed. "Atheists are freethinkers."

"We're not supposed to think freely?"

The pregnant pause. "The term has been hijacked by nonbelievers," Father Gregory said. "We *think* for ourselves, but we seek the *truth* in God."

We turned our attention to Helmut's paper, "From Schism to Ecumenism"—the attempt to glue the shards of the Christian world back together again. He didn't sound too optimistic.

While the rest of us moved on from topic to topic, Eric sat there, floating in the tide, Polaris nowhere in sight.

✸

After an hour in bed to keep up appearances, we silently packed SNAC food, then slipped out of the dorm, down the stairs, and through the change-room door. Outside, the air was cool and moist, the Milky Way a bright splash across the nighttime sky.

As we rounded the church and crossed the lawn, we paused for a moment on the edge of officers' country. We could see the windows of the monks' cells stacked three stories high, stretching out in a little wing from the abbey church. This was as close as any of us had ever been to the cloister.

"I wish I had my binoculars," Jon whispered.

There were lights in several of the windows. The monks' cells, we were told, consisted of a bed, a desk, a chair, a wash basin, and a small wardrobe. That was it. We watched the rooms for a few minutes, our eyes adjusting to the light. We could make out two of the monks, Father Albert and Father Francis. They were sitting at their little wooden desks. When a new light suddenly switched on, we all hit the deck like trained commandos. I could see Brother Thomas plain as day.

"You spy, I spy," I whispered.

Brother Thomas pulled off his habit and then his T-shirt. After opening his wardrobe and pulling out a fresh T-shirt, he hesitated before putting it on. He raised his right arm and took a deep whiff of his pit.

"Oh, *gross*," Eric said.

We tried to stop laughing, but Brother Thomas heard us. He put the new shirt on, approached the window, and peered out into the night. We froze face-first in the grass. He stared hard but couldn't see us with the moon still hiding behind Mount Saint John. Then he closed the drapes, and we quickly scurried away.

It was midnight when we finally took a seat on the edge of the cliff and gazed down at the gold-dust lights of Ennis. We cracked open a six-pack of Coke and passed around a bag of potato chips.

The first order of business was to try to get me to talk about Mary. "Details" were what they were looking for. But I needed to keep something for myself, something completely unconnected to them or to this place, something mine alone. I quickly changed the subject.

"It's common knowledge that in places like Germany and France monks brew beer and wine and all sorts of booze," I said.

"Think about it. They've got a still here somewhere. They just hide it because of the seminarians. I say it's in their rec room." I lit a cigarette, planted it between my lips, and stood with my toes hanging over the edge.

"I heard something at our parish picnic last summer," Jon said. "A former seminarian said there was a coup among the monks back in the 1960s. A huge struggle for control. Half of 'em backed the old abbot and half were looking for an overthrow." Here he paused for effect and threw a stone over the edge. It took a while for it to click on the rocks below. "The last abbot had a heart attack. He was only sixty-three years old. But everyone knows these guys live into their hundreds. He said there was a big cover-up, then someone came out from Rome to calm things down."

"What a load of crap. Who told you that?" Eric squinted in disgust and folded his arms across his chest.

"Same guy who gave me this." Jon pulled an old-fashioned skeleton key from his pocket and held it up in the dim starlight. "The key to the attic."

The attic was one of Saint John's high-security sectors. Seminarians were only allowed up under certain conditions, such as storing or retrieving suitcases on move-in or move-out days, or to rummage through old props and moth-eaten costumes before the Easter Pageant. On these occasions Father Gregory would watch our every move to make sure we didn't venture too far and that each of us left when we were through.

The attic was enormous. It was rumoured to be a continuous passageway connecting each part of the complex. That meant it led out into the monks' wing, where we were never allowed to go. The monastery was cloistered, off-limits to all but members of the religious community. No student had ever been there.

"I was keeping it a surprise," Jon explained. "He was carrying it on his key ring all these years. Like a trophy. Said it should be handed down from generation to generation."

I couldn't believe Jon hadn't told me this before.

Eric spat another mouthful. "Man, you guys are bound for trouble this year, aren't you?"

I flicked my cigarette in his direction. "Lighten up, Saint Eric."

"I'm just telling you," he said. "We're only a month into the semester and you're already losing it."

"Losing what? Do you wanna bet I top the class this year?"

"In what? I haven't heard of any blow-job competitions."

I jumped up and stared straight into Eric's beady eyes. He didn't seem the slightest bit intimidated. Eventually I extended my hand in a conciliatory gesture. The idiot went for it, and I spun his arm around his back and pinned him a few inches above the little tobacco puddle he'd accumulated in the dirt. Connor and Jon yanked us apart and pulled our underwear up mid-chest.

We wouldn't make it up to the attic that evening or the next. Such an undertaking required considerable planning. We slurped up the last of the Coke, stretched out on the blanket, and watched satellites streak across the sky. Eric was convinced that one of them was the space shuttle. No one challenged him because it was more fun to believe. And who knew? It might be true.

✳

Saturday was supposed to be a break from the Big Routine, the one day of the week we were allowed to go into town. I never missed going until now. This Saturday, as well as the following two, would be spent slaving down at the barn with Connor to make up for beating on the Baptists. This, of course, was in addition to regular Saturday chores.

After breakfast I wandered back up to our dorm, crashed on my bed, and flipped through the latest *Car & Driver*. I wanted to take a moment to feel sorry for myself and to read up on the Pontiac Fiero. I had been watching the car's development ever since it was an artist's sketch. This, I said to myself, would be the next VW Beetle. A sporty two-seater with revolutionary plastic side panels and a "mid-engine" design. They would sell millions. I could see myself in a black one.

Todd came in, Adam's apple first. "No bed-lounging—and why aren't you doing housework, MacAvoy?"

"Todd, I'll bet you're a decent guy when you're not in charge of something."

"If you'd just do what you're supposed to—"

"What's your rush? Late for a torture session?"

I felt sorry for him, in a way. He really didn't have any friends, even among the seniors. They just seemed to tolerate him. In return he didn't harass them the way he did everyone else.

"C'mon," he said, "when are you gonna clean the showers?"

"When I feel like it."

He stuck a finger up his nose, then flicked it at me. "Get any off that Ennis girl?"

I sat up quickly. "Don't screw with me, man!"

He glared down at me and sighed, probably hoping I'd take a swing at him and give him an excuse to retaliate. But I didn't oblige. I hated getting hurt.

"I'm working down at the barn this morning. I'm on a tight schedule. I'll try to squeeze it in."

"Punk." Todd turned and left in search of someone else to torment.

※

Housework went in shifts. My turn, along with those of two other guys, had fallen on the showers. The shower room—a giant green tiled chamber big enough for twenty seminarians to use at once— would have to be disinfected and scrubbed from the ceiling down to the drains. There were worse jobs.

I saw them the moment I passed the washing machines and stepped into the change room—three scrawny freshmen huddled around the door of a toilet. The tiny closetlike stall had a vent at the bottom of a tall, narrow wooden door. The kids were listening to whatever was inside. As I approached, undetected, they suddenly looked at one another and grinned. Todd was leaning against the wall down the corridor, palms raised, urging me to stop and keep quiet. One of the kids turned a key and the door slowly, silently, opened. Their laughter couldn't be contained. The boy inside was standing with his pants down around his ankles, bare ass to the world. He was so engrossed he hadn't even noticed. The other kids chanted, "Michael's pullin' his wire. Michael's pullin' his wire."

I laughed, then caught myself when I glanced over at Todd. The twisted fucker had set the whole thing up. He had a talent for bringing out the worst in everyone.

Michael Ashbury nearly tipped over with shock. He immediately pulled up his pants and turned to meet the assault with wild, frightened eyes. As the others giggled and pointed at their classmate, he feverishly buttoned his pants. There was nothing he could say.

I picked up someone's tennis shoe and hurled it at them. "Leave him alone, you little maggots!"

Still laughing and hooting, they raced past the doors of the shower room and down the stairs to the rec room. Michael Ashbury ran in the opposite direction. Todd sauntered over and retrieved the master key from the door. I shoved him. He grabbed me by the collar and pinned me to the wall.

"You're pathetic," I said, trying to break his hold. "Were you abused as a child?"

"Are you sure you wanna start something?"

All the noise brought out Eric and Tom Wolosovic from the showers, mops and buckets at the ready. Eric looked at me. "And where the hell have you been?"

Cooled by the thought of witnesses, Todd let go and took a step back.

"Nazi!" I shoved his shoulder as I walked past. "Get some help before it's too late."

/

NINE

UNCOMMON KNOWLEDGE

Outside the doors of the abbey church, a wall of dense, sweet-smelling fog threatened to push its way in. I knelt in our pew, watching the faithful emerge from the cloud silently, steadily, their faces devoid of life. Inside, everyone prayed with feverish devotion. As soon as the newcomers made it into their pews, they instantly fell to their knees and shut their eyes tight, hands clenched and pressed to their foreheads. But I couldn't pray. No matter how hard I tried to get my mind off the subject, all I could think about was the swelling between my legs.

Then a man walked in. No one else noticed him, but I knew who it was. He was in his early thirties and wore a dark blue suit, a snow-white shirt, and a dark tie. His black oxfords were well polished and he carried a large book under his arm. Despite the disguise, there was no mistaking the long, wavy brown hair, beard, or piercing blue eyes. It was, of course, our Lord.

He sat in the front pew among the kneeling laity, His gaze firmly fixed on me. No one else paid Him any attention, but it was all I could do to avoid His gaze. Finally, as Mass began, He opened his big book and started writing something, pausing every minute or two to look up at me and shake His head in disappointment. My heart bashed against my ribs. I wanted to get up and run away, but my legs wouldn't respond. Desperately I tried to hide the aching lump, to tame my mind and pray, but I couldn't take control. And then I felt a hand on my back, and every muscle in my body seized up.

"William," Jon whispered, buttoning his shirt in the dark. "Wake up. It's time."

Bed springs squeaked ever so slightly as the others rose. Stocking feet against the terrazzo floor made a dull, warm sound. Utterly relieved to be home in the waking world, I kicked off the covers and quickly pulled on pants.

It was 1:30 a.m. With any luck Father Gregory wouldn't make any more of his surprise tours. He liked to appear suddenly, floating between dorms and beds in his silent slippers, hands clasped behind his back, a string of oversize rosary beads swinging like a tail behind him. Although I'd seen him hundreds of times, the sight still gave me the heebie-jeebies.

Connor, the advance guard, took up position outside Father Gregory's cell. He placed his ear to the door, paused, and bent to see if there was any hint of light underneath. Then he looked up and waved us on.

"You guys, I've been thinking..." Eric said. "You know how upset they can get about the attic and—"

"Eric," I said, "give in to yourself. You're here. You want to be here. Shut up and try to have fun."

There was a little red security light above the attic door. This incriminating beacon shone when anyone turned on the lights up there, or was stupid enough to tap into one of the electrical outlets. Clever. The monks were serious about the attic.

The key didn't work at first. It took several nervous minutes of fumbling to get it to tickle the innards the right way. When it did and the door slowly swung open, we all breathed a collective sigh of relief. Then we heard a bang and a muffled thud from around the corner in the nursery. We held our breath, waiting. Silence.

"Stay here," I said. "I'll handle this."

I poked my head around the corner and saw the disturbance right away. Tom Wolosovic was sprawled on the floor in front of his wardrobe, straightening and bending his leg as if it were time for phys ed. Everyone else was still in bed asleep. I double-checked to make sure the light hadn't come on in Father Gregory's cell, then walked over and stood directly above Tom's head. "What are you doing?"

"I fell out," he whispered, rubbing his eyes.

"Of what?"

"The wardrobe."

I looked up and saw that he had modified the tiny space and stacked pillows against the sides. He had crammed himself in there and had somehow fallen asleep.

"My legs are numb," he said. "Help me get back in."

"Why would I do that, freak?"

"I've got a bet going. Seventeen bucks says I can stay in there all night. No one saw me fall out. Help me back in."

"Forget it."

"What are you doing in here?" he asked, propping himself on his elbows. "You're not supposed to be in our dorm, especially in the middle of the night. Help me in and I won't tell."

I stuffed him back into the wardrobe, explaining I was on my way to take a piss when I heard him hit the floor. I told him he was lucky it was me and not Father Gregory. Ungrateful little shit. He was still trying to get comfortable when I shut him in.

The boys were standing just inside the attic door when I returned. "Kid games," I explained, and they rolled their eyes.

"Make sure and lock it," Eric said as Connor pulled the door closed behind me. Flashlights were switched on as we quietly celebrated our first victory of the evening.

Dusty wooden stairs led up into the black. The attic was immense, probably twelve feet high at the peak. It had the same stale air that filled my grandfather's house. We picked our way across the floor, hugging the wall to avoid the creaky spots in the middle. Carefully we travelled past luggage, old chairs, and bed frames until we hit a chicken-wire wall at the end of the section. It was locked. Inside were the Roman soldier costumes and cowboy hats of theatrical productions long past. There was even a big papier-mâché cross and a crown of thorns at the far end of the enclosure. I pulled up a loose section of the chicken wire, near the corner, and folded it back so we could all squeeze through. We did the same on the other side of the prop department and found ourselves in unfamiliar territory.

"We must be s-s-somewhere over the n-n—" Connor tried to say.

"Nursery," Jon finished for him. "I've never been this far."

"No one has," I whispered.

"I guess we have to continue around to the left if we're going to head out over the monks." Eric's newfound bravado surprised us. He took out his tin of tobacco and plucked a wad in the dim flashlight beam. Then, all of a sudden, we heard a thump. "Ow!" he cried.

"Shhh!" Connor hissed. "Can it."

"I smacked my head," Eric explained, rubbing his temple and flashing his light at the offending joist.

A few yards down the attic we encountered a collection of cardboard boxes. Stacked in the same meticulous order the monks applied to the rest of their existence, each box had a typed list of contents and a date on the lid. They went five deep and twelve across on each side of the passageway.

The one I opened first was labelled TAXES: 1947. Inside were well-organized receipts and invoices for the necessities of life on the hill. Flour: one hundred pounds. Motor oil: five cases. Cinder block: two palettes. Eric found old issues of *Western Catholic* magazine, and Connor delved into the *National Geographic*s. Jon's box held something much more interesting.

"Hey, guys, listen to this." Jon scanned the file as I held the flashlight for him. "Peter Tassiek…senior, 1959. Turfed."

"What do you m-m-mean, *turfed*?" Connor asked.

"Expelled, it says, but it doesn't say why," Jon answered.

"So this must be the loser file," I said.

"No, this one's good." Jon studied the page. "Ben Allair, senior, same class. Graduated cum laude. Took the provincial Latin ribbon. Lousy at math, though."

"Is there anything more recent?" Eric asked.

Jon flipped open another box. "This one goes up to 1968."

I opened a box from 1953 and fingered through the grades and student files of a group of guys who had sat at our desks and slept in our beds. Now they were car salesmen, doctors, insurance agents, priests, bums...old. Their last year at Saint John's had only these records to mark their passage. We would make a bigger splash.

"Holy s-smokes," Connor said. "Take a l-l-look at th-this." He pulled out a dark blue ledger from the box. "T-this one's from the 1970s. Medical files for the whole p-place."

Connor read off a roll call of broken arms, stitches, and concussions attached to the names of students, plus biopsies, checkups, and urine tests for the brothers and priests. At the bottom were two names with long lists of charges and dates after them. One was for Brother Andrew. He was a diabetic with a heart condition, and tests and checkups for him were frequent. Insulin, syringes, pills. The other column was for Brother Thomas.

"C-check it out," Connor said. We all checked. The list detailed office appointments with a clinical psychiatrist in Vancouver and a psychologist in Ennis. There must have been twenty appointments. Below that was a list of prescriptions for something called lithium carbonate. "What the hell is l-l—"

"Who knows?" I said. "But it's highly classified shit."

"What?" Eric asked.

"The psychiatrist, Einstein."

"It could mean anything," Jon said.

"Yeah," I said. "Like Brother Thomas is *disturbed*, or maybe even homicidal?"

"M-maybe he's just a h-h-homo."

As we replaced the files, we each thought about what it meant, scanning our memories for everything Brother Thomas had ever said or done in our presence, searching for signs of slipping sanity or a "pattern." With the closing of the last box we sealed the issue between us.

Flashlights blazing into the dusty unknown, we rounded another corner into a long corridor. Off to each side of the attic were more boxes and stacks of red ceiling tile. The monks were smart that way. They were always planning ahead, usually in terms of decades.

There were rolls of insulation and old, frazzled furniture, even worse than the stuff we had in our rec room. Then we encountered a small door. We all saw it at the same time. It was only about five feet high. The flashlights revealed a path in the dust from the main section of the attic to the little door, a sure clue it had been opened sometime in the last century. I tried the knob.

"Wait," Eric cautioned, his whisper barely audible. "This looks bad."

I rolled my eyes, then opened the door. There, up about six steps, was a small room with a desk, a chair, lamps, shelves, and tons of electronic equipment. We closed the door behind us.

"Holy shit!" Jon cried.

The heavy blanket of dust that filled the rest of the attic wasn't present here. This space was well cared for and carpeted. Carpet, for Christ's sake. The only carpet in the entire school was a red rectangle leading up to the altar in the church. I always felt a little strange when I stepped on it on my way to receive Communion. Carpet was something special.

Jon shone his flashlight over the equipment. "What is this stuff?"

"Where the hell are we?" I asked. "I thought the attic was the highest point in the building."

"No," Jon said. "Remember that little point thing that comes out above the monks' rec room? This must be it."

There were no windows in the place to confirm this hypothesis, but it sounded plausible. We decided that what we were faced with, after about five minutes of collective inspection, was a ham-radio unit.

"Have you guys ever seen the antenna for this thing?" Eric asked. "They're supposed to have huge antennae."

"Bell tower!" we chimed in unison.

There were transmission logs dating back twenty years and records of conversations with people in Russia, Hong Kong, Brazil, Scotland, and all over North America. Most of the entries recorded the frequency, time, and date, and a short line or two about what had been said. Mostly things like:

Made contact with Mr. Bains in Inverness, Scotland. Wanted to know if we were able to see the aurora borealis at our latitude... Faint transmission received from Kamchatka Peninsula. Russian Orthodox Church of Saint Bartholomew looking for information on the Second Vatican Council. Father Rostov was given the location and frequency of an operator near Anchorage who speaks Russian. A novena will be said for their well-being...

"Boring shit," I said.

"Boring?" Eric stared back, unbelieving. "This stuff's amazing. What's your problem?"

"Nothing a little lithium carbonate can't cure."

"What?"

I flipped back the ledger to the original page and returned it to its exact position. "Nothing."

Eric and Connor continued on carefully, quietly snooping through the room. Jon stared at the sprawling equipment, thinking. Then he looked at me with a curious expression. He was making high-level contact with my motives and intentions. "That's one major ace in the hole."

"We'd better beat it," I said, checking my new watch. "It's almost three. We have to get a couple hours' sleep or we'll be wrecked."

It was as if we had never been there. All traces of our presence erased, we pulled the door to the radio room closed and then locked the attic behind us. Back in the dorm, as I slipped into bed, Jon gave me that look again, so I gave him the finger.

TEN

THE GATEKEEPER

There were committees for everything. The Fire Committee was the first to fill its ranks. The Breakfast, Lunch, and Dinner Committees followed. The Morning Communion Service Committee never got off the ground due to lack of interest. Camping meant untold opportunities for order to break down, but Brother Thomas worked overtime to control as many variables as possible.

The setting sun dressed the mountains in gold and copper, the cosmetic light smoothing out the scars of roads and clearcuts. The camp spun out from the fire pit in a centrifugal spray of dishevelled tents and disemboweled backpacks to the edge of the cedar forest on one side and the cliff overlooking Ennis Valley on the other. My fire crackled at a healthy rate, indiscriminately blowing smoke in every possible direction. I shared a log sofa with members of the Dinner Committee—Jon and Eric—and watched the hot dogs turn from cold flesh tones to bubbled black in a matter of seconds.

The annual Autumn Trek took us a full twelve miles over abandoned and overgrown logging roads into the mountains behind Saint John the Divine. Most of the underclassmen chose to go, seventy in all. Nearly all the seniors remained behind doing homework and good works.

We had experienced a near tragedy that afternoon and were all feeling a little vulnerable. Victor Gomez, a sophomore, had slid and fallen off the side of the logging road and tumbled thirty feet into some bushes. He was never really in danger of going over the big cliff, where he would have surely been ground to hamburger on the rocks below, but his fall resulted in a few scrapes, a sore knee, and a mild case of shock. It had been strange watching him tumble like that, his heavy backpack stealing his balance, exaggerating the fall. When we finally got to him, he was panting on his back like a helpless turtle.

An eagle soared above our camp, showing little interest in the activities of the sweaty people below. We all looked up and watched it glide effortlessly through the fading sky, not having to beat its wings even once. I shoved another log into the glowing coals. As chairman of pyrotechnics, it was my responsibility, along with my deputies—Helmut and Michael Ashbury—to ensure the fire remained alive as long as it was needed, then make certain it was contained when it was time for bed. I took my responsibilities seriously.

Because Brother Fulbert had a sore throat and had to stay behind, Brother Thomas was our sole chaperon. He didn't really like the outdoors. You could tell he thought he ought to, but out here in the natural world there were too many things that couldn't be managed.

Brother Thomas sat across from me, pretending the smoke wasn't bothering him. He was wearing a green sweater and pants and a grey vest with lots of pockets. During the hike, I had asked him what he was carrying in all those pockets. He had rattled off the inventory: compass, knife, antiseptic, bandages, mosquito repellent, sunglasses, a rosary, holy water, holy oil, a pocket Latin Bible, the Holy Eucharist, and a bunch of other stuff I couldn't remember. He also wore a hat like the one Gilligan had on *Gilligan's Island*.

Brother Thomas got busy steering the Food Committee as everyone lined up with empty buns behind a huge stump that served as a condiment table. His major concern—aside from inspecting hands to make sure they had been scrubbed at the "sanitation station"—was keeping the ketchup knife from entering the mustard, the mustard knife from invading the ketchup, all personal forks and spoons out of the salad, and the salt and pepper shakers together.

Back in the dining hall at Saint John's, when someone wanted salt, you were supposed to pass the salt and pepper together. They were a symbiotic pair that should never be separated. Of all the monks in the abbey, the only one I could imagine enforcing the salt-and-pepper rule on the side of a mountain was Brother Thomas.

He watched intently as one seminarian salted his salad and then passed the pepper to his friend in line behind him. Swiftly he intervened in a controlled, tempered manner as if he was doing it for the first time in his life. The salt and pepper shakers had to be passed together or not at all. I watched this happen three times and pointed it out to Jon, who was sitting next to me. When it was my turn to relinquish the fire and prepare my hot dog, I approached the stump and puttered around, waiting until Brother Thomas was busy inspecting someone's bug bite. Then I grabbed the pepper, carried it to the other end of the stump, hid it behind the applesauce bowl, and sat back down.

Brother Thomas ate last. The first shall be last and the last shall be first and all that crap. He walked over to the stump with his empty bun, and the first thing he did was wipe the mustard knife clean on a napkin. Once he'd built his hot dog, he moved toward the salad. There, right in front, was the widowed salt shaker. He froze and his free hand fell limp. Then he looked down the stump to the right and to the left. Jon tried hard not to laugh as Brother Thomas circled the stump, searching for the pepper. The monk had a peculiar expression on his face. It wasn't anger; it was sincere concern. He set his plate down and circled the stump again, looking everywhere he could think, lifting jars and bowls. Hope in his eyes, he glanced over at the kids innocently nibbling on their charred hot dogs, but the pepper was nowhere to be seen. After that Brother Thomas began seeking out the culprit.

I got up and went for a second helping of salad. Surreptitiously I liberated the pepper from its hiding place, used it, placed it shoulder to shoulder with the salt, and resumed my seat quickly. Eventually Brother Thomas returned to his plate and saw the salt and pepper shakers where they should be. He froze again, staring at them, then reached down and scooped them up. When he turned around, the concerned look was gone. It was replaced with relief.

We couldn't carry a guitar all the way up to our campsite, but Connor's harmonica filled in just the same. After dinner he played some Beatles tunes, and everyone sang along. Brother Thomas sipped his hot chocolate, tossing out recommendations for folk hymns whenever he saw an opening. Finally, when we all lost steam, he said, "I think it's time for rosary."

Beads were pulled from pockets as everyone searched for a soft place to kneel. Brother Thomas started us off, and we all felt warm and connected, repeating the familiar prayers under the shooting stars, the glow of the fire illuminating our pious faces. We were on the fourth Mystery when we heard noises.

Somewhere down the dark logging road flashlights sliced through the night. A couple of men were behind them, broadcasting loud, exaggerated laughter. The volume of our prayers dipped as we peered into the gloom. Everyone, that is, except Brother Thomas.

As the intruders closed in on our camp, their laughter and talk turned to swearing. Just as their flashlights lit the back of one of our tents, Brother Thomas rose, made the sign of the cross, and surveyed our wide, flickering eyes. "Continue," he said, disappearing into the void.

Then, from the pitch-black, a voice cracked, "Looks like the fuckin' Girl Guides to me."

Rosary took on a whole new dimension after that. We felt like potential martyrs kneeling in the wilderness, our faith our only shield from evil. The fifth Mystery was Dean's to lead. He announced solemnly that this one was dedicated to the "visitors."

Brother Thomas's calm monotone could almost be heard above the murmur of the prayers. "Good evening," I think I heard him say.

The men were talking pretty loudly, but I could only make out a few words like *party*, *free country*, and *shit*. "Who the fuck do you think you are?" was followed by a moment of silence. Suddenly Connor got up, crossed himself, and followed Brother Thomas into the darkness. Jon and Eric and a few others looked at one another, wondering if they should stand and follow. A few seconds later Brother Thomas and Connor returned to their places. We all watched the flashlights jab back down the old logging road the same way they had come.

When rosary was over, Brother Thomas announced that our visitors were impaired but seemed harmless otherwise. We were all to go directly to our tents but report any suspicious activity.

Eric and Connor were set up in a little pup tent. Connor dived through the flap, mumbling threats. Jon had a brand-new, lightweight, two-man four-season tent his parents had given him for his sixteenth birthday. I crawled in behind him.

Burrowed deep in our sleeping bags, we recounted the events of the evening and calculated our chances of survival. We speculated that the intruders were Ku Klux Klansmen. In history we had recently learned that the KKK not only hated blacks but Jews and Catholics, as well. We worked ourselves into a considerable panic.

If we were to die here tonight, what would we leave behind? we wondered. What did we have to live for? If they killed us because they hated Catholics, would we be beatified?

I woke up a few hours later to the sound of voices. The slope of the tent had sent us careening into the corner. Jon was practically on top of me, his left arm draped around my shoulder as if I were his wife. I shoved his arm away and said, "Wake up. They're back." He merely rolled over, never breaking his sleep.

The drunken intruders were at the edge of my fire. I watched through the crack in the zipper as they laughed at Brother Thomas. One of them was tall and mostly quiet. He looked as if he was going to pass out at any moment. The other was much shorter and had greasy hair and a scraggly beard. He kept making faces.

I couldn't see Brother Thomas's feaures, but I could make out his perfect posture. The visitors weren't saying anything at the moment, just laughing and pointing at Brother Thomas. Finally the short one breathed in the monk's face and said, "See. I haven't been drinking a goddamn thing."

"It's time for you to leave," Brother Thomas said. "Go in peace."

The tall one didn't react. It was all he could do to stay vertical. The short one made another face as if Brother Thomas's words were the funniest things he'd ever heard. Then he reached into his pocket and offered a bottle to the monk.

Brother Thomas shook his head and gestured toward the surrounding wilderness, signifying their audience with him was over.

"Fuck you, preacher. We were goin', anyway, to sell our souls to the Devil!" They hooted and stumbled off into the night.

I was sure everyone had heard the Devil part at least, but no one made the slightest peep. Brother Thomas stood there for a while until he was convinced they were gone, then returned to the fire. He sat there all night, wide awake, staring into the consuming flames.

The next morning we held a service in the sunshine. The Eucharist had been blessed the day before and transported in a little golden box in one of Brother Thomas's many pockets. He set up a small altar on the stump, complete with bunches of wildflowers, and we knelt around it listening to the readings. Brother Thomas couldn't perform Mass—he wasn't a priest—but he was empowered to hold a Communion service in its place. Although his eyes were red and droopy, he pressed hosts on our tongues with a steady hand. Silently we thanked God for delivering him, and us, from the previous night's evil.

After the service and a clean sweep of the camp, Brother Thomas led us off the mountain and back toward Saint John the Divine. For the duration of that Autumn Trek, he was our one and only hero.

✺

Word of the violation spread across the seminary like the shock wave of a nuclear blast. At ground zero was the seminarians' chapel and its vacant tabernacle. Father Gregory was the first to discover the abomination before the sun came up Monday morning. In his search for a book he'd left behind he ambled past the classrooms, down the steps, and slipped through the side entrance into the sacristy. It wasn't until he was leaving that he noticed the smell. He walked back into the chapel and saw a jumble of papers and mud tracked all over the floor. Hymnals and missalettes were tossed in the pews. Finally his nose led him to the source of the stink. Someone had taken a shit on the altar.

Further inspection revealed that the Holy Eucharist, blessed at Mass only a few days before, was missing. The door of the tabernacle gaped like the open mouth of a corpse. On the back of its little door a pentagram had been scratched into the gold plate. A chalice and candles were also missing.

It was Father Albert's turn to celebrate morning Mass that week. Keeping up a brave face and all the appearances of normalcy, he dedicated the Mass to the conversion of the misguided souls who had broken in and desecrated the chapel. We prayed for their souls and the safe return of the sacrament and chalice. At the moment of consecration Father Albert raised the host high above his head and held it there longer than usual to ensure he was getting God's full attention. We took Communion that morning with a reverence I had never experienced. All of us were bound together with God against the evils of the world.

The police dusted for fingerprints, then we cleaned everything up. The tabernacle door was removed and sent to Vancouver where the pentagram was ground off and the door was replated with gold. The red lantern above the altar was extinguished. God, in the form of the Blessed Sacrament, was no longer present in the sanctuary.

We held a twenty-four-hour vigil for the Satanists, praying in shifts. My turn came from three to four in the morning. It was torture being in the chapel by myself, even with all the lights turned up. The image of the vandals abusing the altar made my stomach ache. What did they look like? Would we recognize them walking up the drive? Did they come to Mass on Sundays and move among us? What sort of sick rituals were they up to? Eric said they'd desecrate the Eucharist and drink human blood from the chalice. I stopped praying for the souls of these fiends and started praying for the hour to pass. By the time Jon shuffled down the steps at five minutes to four, I was already standing, anxious to escape.

The police said they had an idea who it was, but they didn't have any evidence. We all had to surrender our shoes so impressions of their soles could be made to compare with the footprints found outside the window. None of us were suspects, of course, but they had to eliminate all friendly tracks from those that might conceal the hooves of the Devil himself.

A scheme developed among the seminarians to follow the cops around and see who the suspects were. Connor was the chief architect of this idea. We would locate their hideout, rescue the sacrament—if indeed there was any left—and then beat the shit out of the freaks who'd stolen it. Connor had plenty of support, but the obvious challenges of following the cops without being seen, not to mention spending time away from the seminary unnoticed, kept the plans on the drawing board.

It was noted that some cops, when faced with an obvious suspect and no evidence, might let a name slip. That way we could save them the paperwork and mete out justice the old-fashioned way. The underclassmen took up a collection to offer as a bribe, but twenty-one dollars wouldn't really do the trick.

The rage came and went. The cops came and went. The weeks came and went and we were no closer to solving the crime than the day it was discovered. We were left to our imaginations, playing out scenarios of what the Satanists were doing with our God and our chalice.

One certainty survived the rise and fall of emotion: the fact that the pagans didn't have to pry open the tabernacle. It was always locked, according to the monks. It wasn't long before we made the connection to Brother Thomas. He had opened it to bring the Eucharist along with us on the Autumn Trek. The monks were tight-lipped about the entire subject; the code of silence had been imposed. Eric said we should stop the speculation and ask him in person, only he didn't have the balls to do it. Among the four of us—Eric, Connor, Jon, and myself—we played two rounds of Rock, Scissors, Paper to see who would be sent to find out.

When I ambushed Brother Thomas as he walked along the drive one afternoon, I saw the first real emotion I'd ever noticed in him. His expression said that my question was a personal betrayal. He had locked the tabernacle, and insisted he had checked it twice. Someone else must have been in there after we left for the mountains, or they somehow had a copy of the key. He asked if I was satisfied, folded his arms tightly across his chest, and walked back up the hill.

Brother Thomas had even less to say after that. He taught his classes carefully and left without lingering in the halls, preferring to minimize his time with the student body. The tabernacle door came back from Vancouver all shiny and new, and the chapel was rededicated. After a couple of weeks, the whole thing seemed like a scary movie I might have seen but whose plot I no longer recalled.

ELEVEN

A WAKE

I figured it had something to do with my grandfather—the fact that he was gone. I couldn't remember ever picking up the phone to call him. Kids didn't call their grandparents; grandparents did the calling. So it was strange to find myself in the phone booth dialling the number of Saint Theresa of Jesus Nursing Home to speak with Mr. Thorpe.

Because of soccer games I hadn't been able to attend bingo the past couple of weeks and I didn't want him thinking I'd forgotten him, even though I didn't really know the man that well. I also wanted to hear his ideas on what it meant to be a freethinker. I needed to know for myself, and for Eric.

Eric had been spending most of his time in the library, absorbing church history or praying in the student chapel. He'd had several "conferences" with Father Gregory in the Cave. One night during study hall I watched him slowly remove the pictures of the Virgin and saints from the lid of his desk. I didn't question him about it.

Eric wasn't even old enough to shave regularly and he was already having his first crisis of faith.

A nurse picked up on the first ring, someone I didn't know. "Mr. Thorpe, please... William MacAvoy... No, just a friend. Seminary of Saint John the Divine. That's right. I just wanted to—oh...well, does he understand anything? No. That's all right. Well, if you think he can hear, will you give him a message for me? Would you tell him I said hello? And tell him...tell him I'm thinking."

✳

We sat on a lush carpet of moss beneath a stand of Douglas fir on the north side of the Bog. The day had passed us by and the shadows of the forest had thickened, cloaking us in cool silhouette. Sitting in the middle with his legs crossed, Jon rolled out a plastic bag with a flourish as Connor, Eric, and I leaned in to see. "You're supposed to make tea out of it," he said, "but we can mix it with Coke."

Jon had read about nutmeg in a book about life in medieval times. Spices were big back then. They were used for preserving meat, as an anesthetic for operations, for embalming the dead, and for getting loopy. "Let's have a wake," he suggested.

"It can't be a wake," I objected. "He isn't dead yet. It's just a stroke."

"He won't recover." Jon cracked opened a Coke and drank half the contents. Some of it dribbled down his neck and into his white shirt. "His brain is gone. His body won't last long."

Eric gingerly smoothed back his hair into its semipermanent position. "Freethinker... I wonder if he's headed straight to hell."

"Shut the fuck up!" I cried, pointing dangerously between his eyes.

"Don't blame me," Eric whined. "I didn't make the rules."

"He means purgatory," Jon corrected.

Eric leaned back on his elbows. "Nope. Purgatory is for people who are baptized but need to make up for a few sins before going to heaven. And he isn't going to limbo, either. Limbo is for unbaptized babies and Indians who've never heard of God. They can't go to hell, but they can't go to heaven, either. Thorpe's only hope for purgatory is if he gets baptized before he croaks."

My first reaction was to smack Eric in the head. But I knew he was right. The odds were against Mr. Thorpe's admission into heaven. They said a far larger percentage of the population ended up in hell, purgatory, or limbo. But thinking of Mr. Thorpe roasting in eternal flames didn't seem right to me. I couldn't picture anyone in hell, except Hitler and a few mass murderers.

I'd had recurring dreams about limbo and purgatory ever since I was a kid. To me these places were the same. In my dreams it was a round, padded room, much like Barbara Eden's bottle in *I Dream of Jeannie*. There were an infinite number of these small rooms hooked together like cells in a honeycomb, floating in some distant part of the universe. The rooms were comfortable enough, but communication between them was impossible. You simply had to sit there and wait, and wait, and wait a little longer. I could always sense the other people—men, women, babies—sitting in their cells. But I could never contact them.

I watched Jon spoon nutmeg into his can. I opened mine, drank some, then did the same. "He was a smart old guy. I liked him."

"I'm sorry," Eric said finally.

We mixed two teaspoons of nutmeg into our Cokes and drank. It tasted terrible, but to show off Connor plopped a pile directly into his big mouth. We sat around for a while, waiting to be overcome with hallucinations.

"Nothing's happening," I said after five minutes. I shovelled another teaspoon in, swished it around, and finished the entire can. "I don't feel anything."

"Me, n-n-neither," Connor said.

"I don't want to be a priest anymore," Eric announced. He threw his head back and dumped a heap of nutmeg down his throat, then chased it with a big chug of Coke.

Jon and I met the ante with another spoonful. Still nothing happened.

Eric stood and belched. "I respect Father Gregory. He's one of the most intelligent, wisest men I've ever met. He's read everything there is on God and philosophy and religion—you name it. But I don't trust him anymore. I don't know if I trust anything." He picked up a stick and threw it into the smooth mirror of the Bog. The radiating waves sent water spiders dancing. "Who am I to question anything? I'm only sixteen. I'm not that smart."

Jon lay back on the cool green moss. He looked up at Eric's face, studying his pursed lips and serious eyes. "Yes, you are. We're all smart enough. God gave us minds to question."

Eric hugged himself and stared at his shoes. "Yeah, well, I pray to keep from thinking."

"I pray to keep from…" But I didn't finish, and no one seemed to notice.

We waited like that for a time, watching the sky trade blue for black as the quarter moon rose over the Bog. Connor told us the story of his dad's friend who had a son, about our age, who became addicted to heroin. It started off as a party dare. It felt good and the kid thought he was strong enough not to get hooked. He tried it again, and then again and again until it consumed everything— his car, his savings account, the money in his dad's wallet, the gas card in his mother's purse. Other people's stuff could be quickly sold at pawnshops. In order to pay for a fix he even let someone screw him. Then one day the Salvation Army rescued him and put him in a methadone program. God touched him and cured him of his addiction, gave him his life and family back and washed him clean of his sins. He climbed back up. Connor wondered aloud if maybe freethinking was addictive like that, if doubt and maybe even nutmeg were like that, too.

Eric didn't know. No one knew. We all swallowed another big spoonful of the rusty powder, then quietly sneaked back to the dorm. Numb, we crawled into our beds, no farther ahead than when we started.

✸

Connor and I were squeezed tightly onto Jon's bed, trying to keep ourselves together in the midst of a delayed reaction. Eric had somehow disappeared. By two o'clock we were bug-eyed and tripping.

Jon said it felt as if he'd taken a few caffeine pills; his heart was pumping as if he'd just run a race. Connor was disoriented. His blue eyes had turned black, and he had to shield his pupils from the weak moonlight filtering through the window. I sat sandwiched between them, my T-shirt over my head, mumbling prayers through tingling lips.

Around three o'clock I went to the washroom, and when I turned on the light downstairs, I thought I was going to puke. Shaking, I sat on the toilet and wondered what I was going to do. I tried to read the sports section that had been left on top of the tank but couldn't focus on the words. That only amplified my paranoia. I tried to concentrate but forgot the content of each sentence before reaching the end. Frantic, I ran back upstairs to the safety of those trapped in the same dimension.

Sometime after that I woke up and saw Father Gregory pulling Connor's eyelid down with his thumb. "What's wrong with you?" he asked.

The other juniors were already dressing for Mass. I rubbed my eyes but still couldn't focus.

"We ate a banana cream pie last night," Jon said. "I think it was bad." He served up the lie as if it were gospel. It had taken us an hour to concoct the story.

Connor stood up from Jon's bed, looking as if he was going to spew. "I th-think we've g-g-got f-food poisoning."

Father Gregory toyed with the lure, considering it. "Vomiting? Cramps?"

A banana cream pie contained a lot of ingredients that could go bad. We weren't allowed to have a banana cream pie, naturally, and one of us would have had to go to town to get it. We figured copping a plea to a lesser crime might do the trick.

"Mass is in twelve minutes," Father Gregory proclaimed after a few agonizing moments of indecision. "You're going to miss it. Go to the infirmary, get buckets from the hall closet, and wait it out. If you haven't turned the corner by lunchtime, we'll send you to town for a stomach pump."

As Jon led us through the bright confusion, a maze of a place we knew all too well, Father Gregory stopped me and gave me the once-over. His face was unusually bright and smooth, as if he were young again, only flatter. "And how did you end up naked in someone else's bed?"

I was wearing underwear, of course. Father Gregory had a talent for making things sound immeasurably worse than they were. "Sorry, Father," I slurred. "Sometimes I don't have any…pajamas. Oh, I think I'm in my wardrobe."

"Sounds like the salmonella has finally reached your brain."

Eric was found properly buttoned up in his pajamas, kneeling in the Blessed Sacrament Chapel of the abbey church. He had been in there by himself all night, feverishly praying in the dark.

"Something's wrong," he told Father Albert.

Father Albert wiped the sweat from his forehead. "Let's go to the infirmary. You have food poisoning, Eric."

"No, Father, something's wrong…with everything."

Eric kept praying. When Father Albert insisted he get up, Eric began to cry. The priest scooped him up in his arms and carried him all the way back to the infirmary, taking only two rest stops along the way.

✺

After dinner Jon and I huddled over the newspaper in the quiet foyer lounge, trading horoscopes. Refreshed by an eight-hour nap, we were feeling fully clean and sober. Then, without warning, we heard Brother Thomas burst out of the rec room, the doors clattering shut behind him. As he marched upstairs, he looked past us with vacant eyes. His jaw was fixed and his right fist encircled the baton of a magazine. As he disappeared around the landing, Jon and I looked at each other and shrugged. We had just turned our attention to the movie reviews when we heard a bang from up in the toilets.

A small crowd of onlookers assembled. They had come down from the dorms as we ascended from the foyer. Everyone met on the mezzanine outside the washroom, listening, whispering, afraid to go in. Todd finally pushed past the rubberneckers and stepped hesitantly through the open doorway. He walked past the urinals, peered down the row of stalls, and then disappeared from sight.

At that point the flushing began—first one, then another, then the rattle of the handle as the tank ran empty. Connor weaved his way to the door from the rear of the crowd and cautiously stepped inside. Jon and I followed close behind.

Todd stood at the end of the row of stalls. Slowly he glanced at us with wide-eyed apprehension. Farther down we could see the black back of Brother Thomas sticking out from one of the units. The flushing sounded again and then the toilet began to overflow. Brother Thomas stepped out of the stall as if he was surprised at the result. We took a step back, too. He considered us with an empty gaze, seemingly uncertain who we were. We retreated the way we had come, but he pushed past us and out the door without a word.

Todd called for mops as the three of us closed in on the erupting toilet. Shoved down the hole at the bottom of the bowl was the rolled-up magazine. We stared at it for a moment, as if it were a booby trap, then Todd reached down and pulled at the dry end with careful fingertips. When he freed the magazine from the toilet, it sprang open, revealing the glossy smile and generous, dripping cleavage of Terri Welles, 1981's *Playboy* Playmate of the Year.

TWELVE

DRIVES

It was too dark to see clearly. The stink of nervous sweat wafted up from under my arms. I tried to get Mary's jeans off the cool way while we were locked into each other with a blazing kiss. I'd seen it done loads of times in the movies. They made it look like a well-choreographed dance. I finally got her jeans unzipped and thought I was home free. But these were thigh-huggers. She had them on so tight they wouldn't budge past the bottom of her panties. I tried to keep the flow going, but I was working up a sweat attempting to ease them off. Somehow it wasn't working.

We both stood to get better leverage. Mary bent to work her pants down as I took an awkward step closer to lend a hand. I ended up bumping into her head with my stomach and, with the jeans clenched tightly around her knees, she toppled over on the wrestling mat. I laughed, she didn't, and the spell was broken.

"Oh, let's just stop," she said.

"No!" I cried. "I mean, I'm sorry. Let me help you."

"Thanks, but you've already helped enough." She was getting mad, but she finally pulled them off.

As I stood there waiting, I couldn't help wondering that if it took her this long to get her pants off in the heat of the moment, what did she do in an emergency urination situation? Still, they were *très* chic.

One thing my older brother had told me about sex, one important thing he had said in a rare flash of maturity, was "always be a gentleman." He had explained that this not only meant minding your manners and the girl's feelings, it also meant being a *gentle man*. I only remembered this bit of advice once we'd started. But it seemed as if I was doing okay. Mary wasn't complaining or anything, and it only lasted a minute or two. When it was over, I wanted to ask her if she felt anything, if I had done what I was supposed to…if she liked it. But silence felt good. It felt like I loved her. Then she began to cry.

I asked her if I'd hurt her, but she just shook her head. Something else was wrong. I apologized and pleaded and promised I would never do it again. No one ever told me about this. I felt stupid. I felt like the scum of the earth. I reached for her and she hugged me back. We cried together for a while. I kept rocking her, trying to calm her down.

Finally she said, "Stop saying you're sorry. You didn't hurt me. I'm crying because I feel like it was supposed to be something great. Like the best thing in the world. People talk about it all the time. Everyone wants to do it. But it's just…nothing like I was expecting."

Her words sent me into convulsions, and I found myself fighting to breathe. She hugged my head to her breasts, kissed me some more, and told me it was all right. It wasn't my fault, she said. She liked me more than anyone in the whole world and maybe, someday, she might want to try this again.

We made out for a while, our faces flushed and wet, our lips hot and swollen. It felt good to do something familiar. Finally she slipped out of the equipment room when we were sure no one else was around. I watched her disappear down the path through the trees to the Appian Way.

I didn't feel puffed up with whatever it was that was supposed to fill a boy after his first time. I didn't feel as if I'd crossed the threshold into some grand new room of life. I only felt relieved it was over. Then, in the back of my head, I heard a little voice. It reminded me that I wasn't alone in my sin anymore. I had brought someone else in, and that was a whole lot worse. I hung my head and shuffled back across the parking lot, whispering an Act of Contrition.

I was about to take a shortcut through the change room when I saw someone. He had just moved away from the window in the science room above, a black form fading into the shadows.

✸

Hyperactivity Period was held each Friday evening in place of regular study hall. The monks called it Activity Period; "Hyper" was our little addition. What one did with one's time during Hyperactivity Period was limited only by one's imagination and, of course, a long list of well-entrenched regulations and historical precedents. You could do a puzzle, build a model, read, or write. That was about it. We'd rather watch Hawkeye abuse Frank Burns in *M*A*S*H*, which was the Thursday-evening ritual for most people across the country, but that could never happen. Instead, music was our escape.

Down in the rec room Jon was practising his drum-stick twist. He saw the stunned look on my face the moment I entered but quickly averted his eyes. Connor was checking his watch. Eric was busy strapping his base to his skinny body. I tossed my jacket and binder into the pile, walked across the dusty stage, and straddled a stool. Adjusting the guitar strap across my shoulder, I pulled the pick from the strings and began tapping the boards in four-four time.

The fad of the time, the latest strain of pop music in those post-disco days, was known as New Romantic. Bands such as Spandau Ballet, A Flock of Seagulls, Ultravox, and Human League broke ranks with their New Wave cohorts and fused Motown with Glam. The result was eminently danceable tunes with totally forgettable lyrics. They played at androgyny with big hairdos, thick makeup, and outlandish costumes. For some reason the synthetic whine of the New Romantics never quite reached all the way up to the hallowed halls of Saint John the Divine. What did arrive the year before were three boxes of old LPs and reams of sheet music. All of it by the Beatles.

Some woman from the Vancouver Archdiocese was so shaken with the assassination of John Lennon in 1980 that, in a fit of grief, she had packed up her entire music collection and donated it to the student body. Her name, Corrine Daley, was all we knew about her. She would never know the profound effect her gift would have on our musical development, or that she had planted the seed of a new rock-and-roll band. The Band was how we referred to ourselves in polite company. When they weren't around, we were the Virgin Cure, a name that felt especially ridiculous that particular evening.

Michael Ashbury timidly pushed open the doors, dragged a chair to the middle of the floor, and sat with his elbows on his knees. He stared up at us, waiting. I leered back at him. Because he really didn't have any friends among his own kind, he took to shadowing us. Like the quiet, inescapable force of gravity, he was for us *semper ibi*—always there.

"'Back in the U.S.S.R.,'" I announced.

Jon glanced up, ready to assault the drums. Eric stroked the belly of his bass, and Connor stood bowed, waiting to invoke the spirit. Because timing was everything, and because Connor would stutter through the entire countdown, the task of leading the band naturally fell to me. "All right," I said, "one, two, one-two-three-four…"

It was a miracle, really, the way Connor's stutter disappeared when he sang. It made me wonder about the mechanics of it, the blown fuse somewhere in that thick skull of his. What happened to the stutter when he sang? You would think the pressure of singing in front of people would be enough to choke him to death. But when he opened his mouth to sing, only good things came out. I guess it was like the Beatles. Most of the time you couldn't tell the lads were from Liverpool. As soon as the words became music, their accents disappeared.

Although "Back in the U.S.S.R." was just a clever send-up of the Beach Boys' schmaltz, and the irony was completely lost on the monks, there were other Beatles songs that were less cryptic. We hit particular lines with glee, like the one about a guy named Jojo going to Arizona for California *grass*. Then there was that line in "Eleanor Rigby" about Father McKenzie toiling away on a sermon that no one will hear. And the tender *White* album classic "Why Don't We Do It in the Road?" was a personal favourite.

I never quite understood why the monks ignored all those rebellious, unholy lyrics. They didn't allow jeans, gum, girls—anything that made life worth living. At least there was a discernible pattern. Yet miraculously, through some unlocked door at the back of the seminary's moral fortress, rock and roll managed to scratch its way in. It was one of those all too rare situations in which the monks practised their laissez-faire philosophy of "boys will be boys."

One time, I explained this concept to my sister, Andrea, on one of her angst-filled homecomings from McGill University in Montreal. After she was able to soften her grimace enough to form words, she said that this sexist idea was first used to encourage violence in young males, then it grew in concentric circles to justify everything men do—from abandoning their women and children to drunk driving, rape, and war. *Boys will be boys...* From that moment on I decided to use the phrase as much as possible in her presence. We were never very close, Andrea and I.

Jon was shaking his wavy black hair, concentrating on the new drum-stick twist. At the end of a particular flourish he'd snap the stick up and roll it around his hand in midair. He had practised this stunt all summer. The trick would be critical to his budding career as a drummer. Bang, spin, bang—big head shake and crash the cymbals. He looked over at me and smiled. Eric shook his head as he thumped his bass, but his hair, a brown German World War II helmet, stubbornly stayed put. Connor was downstage playing the crowd, which consisted of a rapt Michael Ashbury and three anklebiters trying to sneak in a game of foozeball.

Connor sang about Ukrainian girls and their balalaikas. No one knew for sure what this meant, but we were convinced it was sexy and cool. When the song came in for a landing, all that was missing was the screeching of airplane wheels.

Overwhelmed by what Mary and I had just shared, I nearly forgot to deliver the good news she had brought up for us all: the Virgin Cure had secured its first gig. A group from Ennis High was the dance committee's first choice. They specialized in Duran Duran covers. Three of the five members had come down with mononucleosis, and the committee was scrambling to find a replacement. Mary convinced the socialite-student government types that we rocked. They reluctantly requested our "demo"—all Beatles covers, of course. With no options left to them, they signed us as the headliner of the Ennis High Oktoberfest Dance. No one mentioned, however, that we would never be allowed off the hill—especially for a dance.

"Here," I said. "I made a list." I produced the set list from my binder and passed it around.

"I hope they like the old s-stuff," Connor said. "A l-little h-heavy on the Beatles, isn't it?"

"What else do we know?" I was in no mood to argue. "Plus I don't see a synthesizer sitting around, do you?"

It was almost impossible to concentrate. All I could think about was Mary. I was itching for a smoke, but the monks always stepped up patrols during Hyperactivity Period. Instead, I settled atop the stool and fumbled through the first chords of "Norwegian Wood." Connor looked up from the set list and hit his cue, singing the Beatles' tale of a boy who once "had" a girl who really "had" him. For me the song suddenly took on a personal, prophetic meaning.

The doors at the far end of the rec room swung open. Brother Thomas paused to listen for a moment, his face expressionless. Before Connor could start the next verse, Brother Thomas beckoned me with an inward flutter of his long fingers. I sighed, set my guitar down, grabbed my blazer and binder, and reluctantly followed him upstairs. I could still hear Connor's unfettered voice soaring three stories away.

The room was a crowd of black lab tables. Hooked faucets

hung over the sinks like question marks. An antique periodic table of elements covered the chalkboard, and the place smelled of formaldehyde, vinegar, and acid. Figuring one frog per student since the seminary opened for business in 1911, I quickly estimated that at least two thousand amphibians had spilled their guts in here. Probably more. Enrollment was much bigger before Vatican II.

Brother Thomas wouldn't let me turn on the lights. Instead, he switched on a small lamp on the teacher's desk. I could never figure out why he liked to interrogate me here. He had never taught a science class in his entire life. Walking around to the window, he opened it and sat next to the lamp so that only his black bottom half was illuminated. He rubbed his eyes as if he was tired. "Have a seat, William."

I did as I was told.

"I thought we had an understanding about that girl."

I slumped back into the chair and wondered how in hell he could have known. We had taken precautions this time.

"I know what it's like to be a young man. You boys don't think we're human when it comes to these matters. Well, let me tell you something—we are. We have the same drives as everyone else."

I shifted slightly in my chair.

"The difference is, there's a rule on this hill about having female visitors. What you do on home weekends, on summer vacation, is your own business. Between you and God. But what happens up here is everybody's business—"

"I don't know what you're talking about."

"You're smarter than that. Don't make it worse by denying it."

"Denying what? That I have a girlfriend?"

"Don't take that tone with me." Even in the shadows I could see a muscle in his jaw clenching. "You and Mary O'Brien were fornicating in the equipment room. I saw her sneaking off down the Appian Way."

"That doesn't mean we fornicated, Brother."

"She was where she wasn't supposed to be. If you choose to deny the rest of it, I'm not going to argue with you. The point is—"

"The point is I didn't take a vow of chastity."

He hopped off the desk, took a step in my direction, and slapped me across the face. It wasn't too hard, but it was enough to reestablish the natural order of things. "This is all some kind of joke to you, isn't it? What's come over you all of a sudden?"

I thought of my legal options but quickly remembered that my father had signed a waiver permitting "appropriate and reasonable corporal punishment."

"I'm...sorry, Brother..." I began. "I just have strong feelings for her." My lips still tingled.

"There's a difference between physical urges and emotions. If these *feelings* of yours are more than lust, then they should be built on respect. Shagging a girl in the equipment room doesn't sound like respect to me."

Now I wanted to hit him. How would he know about respecting a woman? Once again my eye caught the periodic table hanging on the wall. I stared hard at the element Li, one of the alkali metals—commonly known as lithium!—on the top-left-hand side.

"Am I making my point here? Life is about relationships, William. Right now you're faced with a choice. You can either keep the relationships you've built with your classmates and the monks, or you can choose to indulge yourself with that girl. I don't care if you have a relationship with her on a proper level, but I can't have you fornicating on campus. It's a mortal sin. You're endangering her soul as well as your own."

I crossed my arms and stared at the floor.

"For your sake I haven't told Father Gregory. We'll resolve this between us. That's all I have to say." He got up, walked out, and closed the door behind him.

I wanted to talk to Mary. I wanted to touch her, hold her. I wasn't about to stop being with her. That wasn't even an issue. I would just have to be smarter, more careful. Instead of calling her I thought a letter might make more impact. The romantic drama of it all. Two young lovers torn apart by the system. Girls loved letters. Maybe I could even be poetic. I sat up, uncapped my pen, and reached for my binder.

When I opened it, I saw right away that it wasn't mine. Just about everyone at Saint John's had the same black binder with the seminary's coat of arms. I must have grabbed the wrong one by mistake when I left the rec room. A French vocabulary exam was in the pocket with an A- at the top. Next to it was Jon's name. I scanned it to see where he had gone wrong.

Written in his dramatic, scrolling handwriting, the vocabulary was perfect. He had scored almost as well on the translation of a short article from *Paris Match* magazine. Better than I had done. When I put the quiz back in the pocket of the folder, I noticed something shoved way down in the corner. I pulled it out and unfolded a big picture of Michelangelo's *David* that had been ripped out of a book. There he stood in all his athletic, naked glory. No caption or words of any kind, just this reproduction of one of the world's most famous works of art. The perfect boy/man who slew Goliath—without so much as a jock strap. Hidden away in the intimacy of Jon's homework, it wasn't art. It was porn. I folded it and put it back exactly the way I had found it, eager to get the thing out of my hands.

Then I noticed something sticking out of a crack in the plastic seam that joined the binder together. I hesitated for a moment, then stuck my finger in and pulled it out. It was the Polaroid from the Cave, the picture of Father Gregory's office chair and Tom Wolosovic's out-of-focus, overexposed stiffy.

✳

After walking past the playing fields and the butternut tree, down the drive and back again, I laid in a course for the chapel. I had missed evening rosary by half an hour. Everyone else was studying or had retired to the dorms. I strode down the quiet corridor and slowly descended the stairs, with Jon's notebook tucked under my arm. The lights were still on and, as I dipped my fingers into the holy water, I glimpsed Jon alone, kneeling in the juniors' pew, rosary beads dangling from his fingers. He didn't look up.

I genuflected and sat beside him. My black binder was lying between us, its white coat of arms facing heavenward. The coat of arms was an open book—representing the Bible and knowledge—at the base of a cross. Above that was an eagle, the symbol of Saint John the Divine, the disciple whom Jesus loved. Below the cross were oak leaves and the letters UIOGD. Underclassmen got their first Latin lesson with these letters. All students took four years of this dead language at Saint John's, and by the time they were out a year or two they forgot most of it. Except this: *Ut In Omnibus Glorificetur Deus*—that in all things may God be glorified.

I placed Jon's binder on top of mine and knelt next to him. After a long few minutes, he slipped the rosary beads into his pocket, hung his head, and slumped back into the pew.

"Don't you have something you want to say to me?" he asked.

I thought a long while before answering. About a dozen different things presented themselves as possible responses: "Have you been staring at my dick in the shower all these years?" "Why are you always around when I'm changing?" "Why were you sleeping so close to me on the Autumn Trek?" And when we were up in the bell tower: "If this gets out, what will people think about me?"

"You stole my binder," I finally said. "Don't ever do it again."

He stared at me, a questioning look in his eyes. Then he bowed his head. "Bill, if you saw anything in there that seemed weird..."

I felt I had to say something, but I didn't want to believe it. And I didn't want him believing it, either. "I saw a stupid picture. So what?"

He looked as if he was about to cry. "I'm so confused, Bill. I don't know—"

"You don't know *shit*." The moment the word left my lips I regretted the blasphemy in front of the Blessed Sacrament. I waited for the poison to disperse, then I whispered, "It's just a stupid picture. It doesn't *mean* anything."

"Bill, you're the best friend I've ever had." He was just on the dry side of letting it out. "I've got to talk to someone about this. I've been in here praying for the guts to tell you. I can't tell the monks."

"Tell what? There's nothing to tell." More than anything in the world I wanted him to deny it, explain it all away.

"Yes, there is." He sat next to me, the binders hiding the evidence between us. "I don't know what's wrong with me."

"There's nothing wrong with you."

"Bill, I'm interested in things…people…I'm not supposed to be."

"That picture means nothing. I don't want to hear about that stupid picture. You were keeping it for a joke. Blackmailing Wolosovic. And that statue—you were probably keeping it to compare yourself to. You know, to work out certain muscles so you can look like…" It was a pathetic attempt, but it was an attempt.

"I…I sometimes I…" That was it. He was crying. Hot tears slid down his cheeks, but no sound came from him. He barely even blinked.

"You're not queer, Jon. And don't psych yourself into thinking it."

Tears fell onto the knees of his pants, making little black marks on the material. "This place is driving me crazy. I'm so alone."

"No, you're not. We're all here together. You and me. And Connor and Eric. We're brothers. We're a unit."

"This is *different*! You're different. I'm not like you, Bill. I'm not so sure of myself all the time. I have doubts about things and I can't…I just want to be…"

"Look, man, women *love* you. You're the best-looking guy in the school. I think Mary first started hanging around after Mass because of you. You're just in a phase. You're shy."

"You don't understand."

"No, I don't. And you don't know what you're talking about." I stood and grabbed my binder from beneath his. "Look, I know you. You're confused, that's all. Don't make it something it's not. Now let's go back to the way things were and forget this."

I walked to the front of the chapel, genuflected to the Blessed Sacrament, dipped my finger in holy water, and made the sign of the cross. *In the name of the Father, the Son, and the Holy Spirit…*

"Bill…" Jon croaked, almost pleading. "I've got to tell you something. I'm not finished yet."

I turned and pointed my still-wet finger. "I'm serious, man. You are *so* confused. You're just really lucky I'm not taking this the wrong way. If you know what's good for you, you won't talk about this ever again."

He thought for a second, then wiped his face. "What time is it, Bill?"

"What? Who cares?"

"What time is it?"

I pushed the button on the watch he had given me. The red numbers glowed to life. "It's 10:20. So what?"

"Remember it. Ten-twenty. I want you to remember because it's the time I tried to tell you the truth and you wouldn't listen." He sat up straight. "You'll see it on the clock twice a day, you'll see it in addresses, you'll hear it in phone numbers—every time that number comes up you'll remember. And so will I. Ten-twenty, Bill. Ten-twenty…"

I thought he was losing his mind. I stood paralyzed for a moment, hesitating on the border between fight and flight. "That night up on the bell tower…"

He stared at me as if I'd stabbed him with a javelin, eyes blinking, red and vacant. I waited a little longer, then turned and left him there.

As I walked to the dorm that night, I said a prayer for Jon, and then one for the rest of us.

THIRTEEN

CONFIDENCE MAN

Brother Fulbert always made us finish soccer practice with wind sprints. We hated him for it. We'd stand there with our hands on our hips, panting after putting in an hour's work. No coasting in for a smooth landing after playing a hard scrimmage. Passing, shooting, defensive manoeuvres—everything done with gusto. Now we were lined up for what seemed like an insult.

The faded chalk lines of last year's football field were used for only one thing that fall: wind sprints. Flag football was only played in the spring. And only for fun. Real football called for size, strength, and tons of expensive equipment. These were all in short supply at Saint John the Divine, so we concentrated on soccer. But the yellowing yard lines came into sharp focus after soccer practice each day when Brother Fulbert stood in his ratty blue track suit and jerked his arm down to signal the start of the set.

It was an unusually warm afternoon, a stray bit of summer lost at the end of October. I was covered in sweat. I would have merely loped along and not worried about where I placed if Connor hadn't been so absolutely sure of himself all the time. But he was. He crouched down, then sprang into action. I had to try. I had to keep up with him.

Connor bowed his head and ran as if his life depended on it. A short couple of yards, then down to touch the chalk line and back again. Touch and then out again, a little farther along the torturous gridiron. Connor reminded me of the Six-Million-Dollar Man when he ran wind sprints. I could almost hear that high-tech electronic pinging from the TV show. I'd burst my lungs trying to catch him.

When it was finally over, I tumbled onto the grass in an exhausted heap. I lay there looking at the blue sky, sucking up great volumes of oxygen. Connor bent over me, hands on his knees, smiling. There was nothing to say, so he straightened, gave one of his President Nixon salutes, and made a little victory dance.

While everyone else wandered back to the showers, Connor, Eric, Jon, and I headed for the Bog. It was much too late in the season for a dip, but it was sunny and the dare had been building since breakfast.

There was a place near the row of blackberry canes where you could strip and dive in at the corner of the Bog without being seen from the seminary or monastery above. Once you were in the water, it was okay. No one could tell you were skinny-dipping.

Eric kicked off his cleats, shed his clothes, and slowly waded in. He let out a squeal as the cold reached his firmly cupped testicles. Connor followed, diving in and staying under for a few seconds. When he surfaced, he didn't cry out, but I could tell how cold it was by the way he gasped. I was fighting the knot in my shoestrings when Jon finally caught up. He hadn't muttered a word all practice. He stood over me, hesitating. "I'm going in for a shower. I'll see you guys later."

"Wuss," I said.

"I just don't feel like swimming."

"Why not?"

Jon glared at me for a moment, then blinked. He wouldn't even look at Connor and Eric. "I just don't."

Eric was calling out for us to join them. Connor was splashing so much water in his face I could hardly see him. Then I noticed that, for the first time since I'd met him, Eric's silver scapular medal was no longer hanging around his neck. It was almost as if he were missing an ear or his front teeth. He looked up and yelled, "C'mon, get in here! I need some backup *now*!"

Jon turned and jogged up the hill.

⚜

We sat around the table in the dark, musty typing room, trying to keep our poker faces. It was Eric's turn to deal.

The typing room was one of those special little chambers at Saint John's that had been built with a specific purpose, given an appropriately descriptive name, and then never used as intended. No one ever typed anything, anywhere, in this school. Nevertheless, the room had a shelf running along three of its four walls, with electrical outlets spread apart wide enough for ten students to type at the same time. As if. There was one typewriter in the room, it wasn't electric, and it didn't have a ribbon. The room was used exclusively for poker on Wednesday afternoons. We called it the Casino.

"What's the game?" I asked, cracking open a can of Coke.

"Five-card draw, suicide kings wild." Eric finished dealing, reached for his empty Coke can, and spat a string of brown goo inside.

"That's disgusting," Connor said as he focused on his new cards. "What?"

"The sound of you spitting is making me gag. Why can't you s-smoke like n-normal people?"

"Smoking is wrong," Eric replied. "It will kill you."

Connor looked up on the discard. "And s-sucking on that stuff till it gives you m-mouth cancer is okay?"

"The monks don't say anything about it."

"Is that the way you decide what's right and wrong?" I asked.

125

"What?" Eric looked around the table. "Are you guys ganging up on me?"

Connor sighed. "Where's Jon?" The question was aimed at me.

"I don't know."

"What's his problem these days?" Eric asked.

"I haven't the foggiest," I said.

"B-bullshit," Connor muttered, motioning for two cards. "You two w-wear each other's clothes."

My stomach muscles tightened. "One."

"And dealer takes two."

We surveyed our new cards and made the best of what we had. The first round of betting went around the table. Penny ante, fifty-cent maximum bid.

"W-what was he goin' on about down at the Bog?"

"He said he didn't feel like swimming," I said. "That's it."

"He looks like someone died," Eric said. "He won't tell me anything."

Connor stared straight at me, hoping it would unnerve me enough to cough up some more information. "William?"

"He won't talk to me, either, okay? Listen, why isn't Todd here yet?"

Resistance to the Senior Senior's rule had been building throughout the seminary. One of the sophomores had even placed a mouse under Todd's cup at dinner a couple of nights back. After the blessing was said and everyone sat down, the Senior Senior lifted his cup from its saucer and the little grey terror scurried into his lap, across the floor, and out the door. He flung his chair back and turned a particular shade of purple-red no one had ever seen before. Everyone gutted themselves laughing. Todd was going to get even with the unnamed terrorists by scoring reprisals on the student body at large. The Senior Senior would leave no lint unswept, no toilet unscrubbed, no bed unmade. We were ready to take a little money from him.

"All of it has to go to the missions," Eric proclaimed.

The missions were a mysterious, nondescript Catholic charity that always seemed to benefit from Saint John's fund-raising efforts.

No one knew anything about them. I was convinced they were a clever embezzlement scheme hatched by the monks. I thought we should put the winnings into the SNAC coffers.

"We're not going to keep it," Eric said. "It wouldn't be right."

"Todd's a dink and needs to go down," I said.

"But we can't keep the money," Eric insisted.

"Okay, whatever."

"Shut up," Connor whispered. "They're c-comin'."

Jon entered the room with Todd in tow. If Todd could have only seen over his ego, he'd have spotted an ambush. Jon sat next to me, and Todd took a special, preordained chair next to Eric and directly across from Connor. So far so good.

"So," Todd said, "I hear you kids wanna learn a little poker."

"We only know one game so far," I said with a straight face. "Show us how the seniors play."

We started with a little five-card draw and stud. Wild cards and straight up. Then we played Chicago, Boston, and Spit in the Ocean. Todd was teaching us about cards and life. He was winning at both. We gave him a Coke and passed around some Smarties. All was right with the world.

Every time Todd dealt, he did this little thing with the cards when he cut the deck. He held it out in front of him and cut it one-handed. It was smooth, but not half as impressive as he thought.

"It's great to escape the imps for a while," Todd said. "They're driving me crazy." He opened his Coke, guzzled half of it, and let out a noxious belch. "I mean, I got little brothers back home, but they were raised right. Not like street urchins."

"Uh-huh," I grunted.

"They've been g-g-givin' you p-problems?" Connor asked.

"Let's just say if they were my brothers, there'd be asses kicked around this place pronto."

After we played for half an hour, we slowly exchanged glances around the table. The cards were about to sour for old Todd. The scam went like this...

There was only one piece of "art" hanging on the walls, a picture of Saint Francis of Assisi, patron saint of touch typists and hard-luck gamblers. The print and frame were two feet square and very dark. Saint Francis wore a black robe in the painting and was surrounded by the dark foliage of a stretch of woods near his native Assisi. He was preaching to a gathering of little black birds. It was all so wonderfully dark and covered in a cheap, reflective sheet of glass. Saint Francis was fastened to the wall by a long stretch of wire and, when supported from below with a couple of pins to angle the image our way, he made a heavenly mirror. The picture, table, and chairs had all been strategically positioned an hour earlier to take into account the lighting and Todd's position and height.

One, two, three times the dealer's deck made its way back to him, and he was beginning to get a worried look. He would either fold or bet the hell out of every hand that came his way. Before it got too far along, Todd said, out of the blue, "Hey, man, sorry about the thing with you and Mary in the gym. I was just goofing around. Shoulda left you two alone."

My surprise was difficult to mask. "Don't worry about it, Todd."

"Well, anyway, sorry, man. I've had a lot on my mind lately."

Too little, too late. We were about to go in for the kill when Todd noticed Jon slowly, almost imperceptibly, glance at the wall above his scalp. At first Todd merely gave his usual stupid smirk and kept counting his change. But then, in a rare moment of lucidity, he stopped, swung his head around, and glimpsed his own sorry face in the shrubs of Assisi.

"Todd," Connor blurted, "you w-w-want some more S-Smarties or s-s-somethin'?"

"Don't move, you shits." He stood and reached out to touch the picture. The pins fell out of the wall, and Saint Francis made a mad clatter against the cinder-block wall as he came to rest in his preferred position. We didn't move. Todd swooped around, pulled down everyone's pile of coins, and swept them over to his side of the table. "Who do you punks think you're playin' with?"

We didn't know.

"Here I am trying to be friendly with some of you younger guys and all you do is try to rip me off. Screw yourselves."

Todd's eyes narrowed, his nostrils flared. Then he reached

down, grabbed his Coke, and took a big swig. Only it wasn't his can. Eric noticed it first, and his arms went limp and his mouth popped open. Todd held his mouth closed for a second, wondering what had gone wrong inside, then spewed Eric's spit onto the floor. A big brown string dangled from his lower lip, then connected his chin and shirt. We hadn't planned this; it was better than anything we could have imagined.

"Fuck!" Todd wiped his mouth and spat again, then went after Eric, who quickly crawled under the table.

While the rest of us were still reeling with shock, Connor burst out laughing so hard he had to hang on to the table to maintain his balance.

"What's so funny?" Todd demanded. He rinsed his mouth out with real Coke and spat it at Eric under the table.

Connor was now holding his stomach and pointing at Todd.

"I said, what's so fuckin' funny?"

Connor chuckled some more, then said, "You w-wouldn't know comedy if it crawled up your l-leg and b-bit y-y-you on t-the ass."

We all lost it then.

Todd lunged across the table and grabbed Connor by the shirt. "Are you trying to get me mad?" He cocked his fist as if he was going to strike.

To calm his stutter, Connor whispered quietly, "Take your filthy hands off me or I'll have to kick the shit out of you in front of the whole goddamn school."

Todd stared hard for a few more seconds, then gave the smiling Connor a good shake before letting go. He scooped up his fair share of the loot, and a lot more, then knocked the remaining pennies onto the floor. As he ran out the door, he looked as if he was going to cry. We could hear his flat feet flapping down the hall all the way past the Cave.

Eric crawled out from under the table and brushed himself off. He reached for his Coke-can spittoon to deposit the juice he'd accumulated during all the high drama. Holding the can at waist level, he dribbled the spit perfectly into the little hole three feet below. It made a tinny plop, and we all laughed as if it was the funniest thing we'd ever seen. Jon did an amazing impression of Todd choking on Eric's spit, and Connor raised his arms in a victory salute.

We were picking up change and congratulating ourselves on our cleverness when Jon gave me a friendly shove on the shoulder. Relieved to see him smiling back at us—at me—again, I wanted to put my arm around him. But then we both remembered, and everything was ruined.

A few minutes later we heard the flip-flop of Todd coming back down the hall. "SS approaching," Eric hissed.

The Senior Senior poked his flushed face into the room. "Oh, by the way, dickheads, I heard your little band is planning to take the school's equipment off the hill to play at the Ennis dance. Fuckup number one—it's not your equipment, it's the school's. Fuck-up number two—you're not allowed to go to any Ennis High functions. Do it and you're history."

FOURTEEN

KNIGHTHOOD

Home Weekend was a chance to savour real food, bask in the warm glow of television for a few days, sleep in, skip Mass, and otherwise see what the hell we'd been missing. Like most of the other guys, Eric was headed home to his family in Prince Rupert. Because Calgary was seven hundred miles away, I'd be homeward bound only for Christmas. And, because Jon's folks were usually too busy—away on buying trips or at their condo in Maui—most of our Home Weekends were spent with Connor at his house in Victoria.

The invitation came, as it always did, on the Monday before the big weekend. Connor's mom would make a point of calling and speaking with Jon and me personally. She made us feel like honoured guests and members of the family simultaneously. "You know we'll be expecting to see you this weekend," she'd say. "We're looking forward to having our boys home," and so on. She was the mother of our home-away-from-home.

That Friday was spent like any other—in classes and soccer practice. But by the time lunch rolled around, the herd of students had noticeably thinned as station wagons pulled up and smiling mothers and proud fathers collected their sons. There was always a moment or two of consideration on the parents' part to see if they could detect any signs of physical or emotional maturity in their boys. Everyone seemed to leave satisfied.

The clink of stainless-steel cutlery against cheap china filled the half-empty dining hall. A lunch of deep-fried halibut, french fries, and chocolate cake was set before us by five students in white aprons. We always got something decent before we were sent home. The monks must have thought they could buy us off with one good meal, that it would somehow erase the gastronomic crimes of previous weeks.

Under a lamp in the corner Eric sat enthroned on the reading chair. We weren't allowed to talk during lunch or dinner. A carefully selected volume of propaganda—usually the biography of a saint, a papal bull, or some other text that had the mark of the *nihil obstat* and *imprimatur* of the Vatican censor board was read aloud in a monotone.

Eric was on the last day of his weeklong stint as table reader. He was reading a book of etiquette published in the 1930s, something about how to treat a woman: let her extend her hand first in greeting, place yourself between her and the traffic when walking along a busy street, stand up when she enters the room, make sure she's the first to sit, and so on. I knew we were being brainwashed, and I made sure none of it sank in. Every other page or so Eric would stumble over a word, stop, get up, and walk over to Father Gregory to find out how to pronounce it and what the hell it meant.

During one of these breaks, Tom Wolosovic started making kid noises at a table on the other side of the dining hall. His tablemates burst into laughter. Father Gregory, who had been following the situation with his extrasensory radar, never looked up. With his free hand he grabbed his little bell and rang it in the direction of the disruption. Tom grimaced sourly, pushed his chair out, and obediently knelt on the floor. He finished his meal in this uncomfortably ridiculous position, and didn't make any more kid noises.

When Eric's drone started up again, Jon leaned over and whispered something to Connor. He said he wasn't coming with us to Victoria.

"What d'ya m-mean?" Connor whispered back. "What are you g-g-gonna d-do *here* for th-three days?" Father Gregory glared at us until we were silent.

Jon shrugged. "My sister and her fiancé are coming up to take me to dinner." Although the prospect wasn't nearly as exciting as spending the weekend with Connor and me, he tried to make the best of it. "Her fiancé goes to UCLA. You should see this guy's Corvette."

"Suit yourself," Connor said, trying to look nonchalant.

After lunch Connor and I finished packing and I went to find Jon. He wasn't in the gym, rec room, classrooms or the Casino. I wandered downstairs to the chapel entrance, and Jon glanced up as I dipped my fingers in holy water. He was kneeling in the pew, praying.

I hesitated, wanting to convince him to come with Connor and me, to be part of the fun we were going to have that weekend. To be part of us again. I wanted to say something to tear down the weird wall that had gone up between us. But I just stood there. He looked up at me with raised eyebrows, waiting for something to happen.

"Have a good weekend," I finally said, then turned and bounded up the stairs.

A little later when Connor and I were consulting the bus schedule, my father called. I hadn't heard from him in over a month. He used to call every Saturday when I first started at Saint John's, back when I was a kid. I guess he figured I didn't need so much checking up on, advice, or direction anymore. It sounded as if he was calling from a pay phone by the side of the road. He told me he was on his way to see me. He hadn't been up to Saint John's since Parents' Day at the end of grade nine. I had made my own way back and forth ever since.

I was going to explain the whole Home Weekend thing to him,

the plans with Connor and his family, but I didn't. Instead, I went upstairs, tossed my duffle bag onto the bed, and told Connor he would have to go home without me.

My dad showed up late that night, around nine o'clock. He wore his one and only suit and tie—a black poly-wool thing. It was off the rack, and came out of its plastic garbage bag whenever there was important union business, a wedding, or a funeral. It always smelled of dust and Old Spice. His black wingtips were older than I was but were still in reasonable shape. He exchanged quick pleasantries with Father Gregory on the front steps and said he was taking me out for dinner in Ennis.

"We had dinner at 5:45," Father Gregory said, looking at his watch. "But by all means, go." Then, reaching into one of the hidden pockets in his habit, he produced a set of keys and handed it to my father. "Please make yourself at home in the guesthouse, room 212. And come down and have breakfast with us after Mass. Perhaps we can go for a walk."

※

There was one decent pizza place in all of Ennis, and my father took me there. I only had a few slices; he barely ate.

"You look good," he said. "How are your grades?"

"Too early to tell for sure, but I'm hoping a little better than last year."

Nervously he lit a cigarette and leaned back in his chair. "I'm on my way back from Toronto. Union business. I wanted to stop by and see you on the way home."

"Ennis isn't really on the way back from anywhere."

He smoothed his hair against his skull the way a man should, as if he was shoving the annoying stuff aside. I always tried to copy that gesture. It looked so much more masculine than the primping and teasing Eric was always doing. "Bill, you're a young man now. I can hardly believe it sometimes."

"How's Mom?"

I already knew how Mark, Andrea, and Linda were doing. They

called to check up on me now and then. Mark was getting stoned a lot and was practically living with some chick in his dorm room at college. My parents would flip if they knew. The girls sent me Care packages with cookies, candy, and greetings from them and their respective husbands. They seemed more like doting aunts and a wild uncle than a brother and sisters. But the age difference had its advantages.

"She's the same as always," he said. "She's doing all right."

He hesitated, and I took another slice of pizza.

"It's been difficult for her with all you kids gone," he continued. "She's going through some adjustments. We both are."

The restaurant was Greek. There were wallpaper scenes of Mediterranean islands and wine bottles with dried grass woven on them. The music had bizarre moaning in it. For a moment I felt as if I were someplace else. A foreign place with old buildings falling apart and a history so huge it made everything we were doing seem insignificant.

"We're not doing so well in soccer this year," I said. "Like always. And I guess I already told you about the dedication of the new abbey church."

He bowed his head, took a deep breath, and sucked up a long pull on his cigarette.

"I've been playing the guitar you gave me. We've got a band, me and Jon and the boys."

He had brought the guitar home one day not long after I caught him on the phone with the woman. A gift of music for my silence.

"It's been hard on both of us, Bill. It's an adjustment. For the first time in twenty-five years we're alone together."

"Well, now you guys can go on romantic vacations and stuff and not worry about us anymore."

The waitress wanted to know if we needed anything else.

"Have an ice cream," he said. "Get him a sundae." When she left, he said, "You're not hearing me, Bill. You're a young man now and you're old enough to understand some things. I wanted to see you before I went home. I wanted you to know there are going to be…adjustments."

"Are you still a knight?" I asked.

"Of Columbus? Yeah, why?"

"It's good to have a knight in the family. You've been a knight as long as I can remember. When I was little, I told the other kids about you. 'My dad's a knight,' I'd tell them. I loved that."

My father's eyes turned glassy red, and he occupied himself with lighting another cigarette. I ate my chocolate sundae with rainbow sprinkles on top.

When I closed the front door of the foyer, it echoed through the empty building. All the lights were out. I walked down the hall to our darkened classroom, sat in the big windowsill, and looked out over the gloomy fields surrounding the Bog. Taking out a cigarette, I lit it, inhaled a long drag, and blew the smoke into the classroom, chuckling to myself.

The sound of someone coming down the hall was barely audible. I couldn't hear Father Gregory's squeaky shoes, but he could have changed to his slippers. After all, it was late. I held the cigarette in my hand and prepared to face whatever I was about to get for smoking inside the school.

When the door opened, I couldn't tell who it was, but it wasn't Father Gregory. It wasn't even an adult. I stared at the figure until my eyes adjusted. "Assberry?"

"What are you doing here? You're supposed to be gone."

"I'm staying for the weekend. What are you doing here?"

"I'm always here on Home Weekends. Are you smoking?"

"I want some time to myself, so why don't you run along and get back into bed?"

"What's wrong?"

"Nothing's wrong. I want to smoke my cigarette in peace."

"Was that your dad?"

"Geez, you're a nosy bugger. Yes. Good night."

"Are you sure you're okay? If they catch you with that cigarette..."

I took another drag and blew the smoke at him. "I'm swell.

Peachy-keen. Thanks for asking. Good night."

"You don't have to be mean."

"I'm not…" My eyes stung and I felt my face flush. "I'm not going to let this place get to me. I'm not going to let anything get to me."

"Me, neither."

He leaned against the sill and looked out over the fields with me. I handed him a cigarette, and he put it to his lips with clumsy hands. He told me it was his first. I lit it for him.

FIFTEEN

EYE OF THE TIGER

Top Forty dance hits flooded the dim cafeteria with pulsing, synthetic strains. Out on the floor guys were doing the stiff one-two and awkwardly ogling the female forms. The girls were gyrating all arty and cool, never once looking at the shiny, eager faces directly across from them. It didn't take much imagination to figure out why Mormons, Baptists, and Benedictines all had a thing against dancing. We sat huddled in the kitchen, staring out through the food-service slot, considering what it was we were about to do and what it had taken for us to get here.

To begin with, Todd had to be silenced. We had begged, grovelled, and generally humiliated ourselves. A convincingly humble Connor had apologized for the Saint Francis poker scam. He had even gone as far as to promise we would help Todd change his image. We'd show our support for him and would do our best—we had sworn on a Bible for that part—to set an example by never talking back to, plotting against, or showing any disrespect for the Senior Senior.

Unfortunately Oktoberfest fell one week after Home Weekend. So, to cover our absence, our stories had to be fleshed out and well rehearsed. Eric and Jon asked for permission to camp out with the portable telescope on Mount Saint John, away from the campus lights. They said they wanted to photograph stars, which Eric had conveniently done at home the weekend before. Connor said he finally had an appointment with a special dentist in Vancouver—an impressive-sounding "maxillofacial surgeon"—to remove his wisdom teeth. That would require him to stay at home overnight. When the monks checked his mouth upon his return, as they were likely to, he would say he got bumped in favour of an emergency case.

My plan was the riskiest and the least inventive. I paid Michael Ashbury seven dollars to stuff his own bed and move into mine for the night. He said Father Gregory never really checked his bay of the nursery during nightly rounds. Plus, he thought it would be exciting to sleep in the juniors' dorm, as long as I promised to change the sheets before his arrival.

We were so focused on getting our act together that we nearly forgot to make arrangements for a place to spend the night. Luckily Mary came through at the last minute with her father's workshop behind the house. We could crash there on sleeping bags and foamies as long as we cleared out before her father woke up. He didn't want to hear or see us.

Another cause for concern was the pressing matter of our "image." Except for Jon, we didn't own any of the cool clothes they wore at Ennis High—expensive jeans, Adidas running shoes, velour and terry-cloth shirts—so we decided to take the crests off our blazers and wear our school uniforms instead. If we wore the same suits and combed our hair funny, we figured we could pass for the Beatles in their *Ed Sullivan Show* debut.

We waited for half an hour like that, Connor singing softly to himself, Eric staring out at the girls grooving and spinning around the floor, Jon grimly focusing on the empty stage. Silently I kept going over chord changes while muttering Our Fathers and Hail Marys. Eventually the hip young deejay nodded his highly sprayed coif and pointed our way. It was time. We stumbled to our positions onstage, not really knowing how to stand or where to look.

"All right, people, hope you're havin' as much fun as I am. We've got a very special treat for you this evening. Fresh from the recording studio, Johnny Carson, and a sold-out European tour, one of the Island's number-one underground bands. Ladies and gentlemen, boys and girls, let's give a big Ennis High welcome to the Fabs!"

We held our breath as the tide of applause washed our way. Eric and I fumbled through the first guitar licks, and Connor fidgeted with the mike, trying not to look directly at the crowd as we launched into "Twist and Shout."

Our new moniker, the Fabs, wasn't my idea. That was Eric's brainstorm. We were told in no uncertain terms that the Virgin Cure wouldn't appear on the posters above the lockers in the hallways. Nor would the Virgin Cure be on the banner behind the stage. I was so disgusted at not being able to use our real name that I was no help trying to come up with a new one.

As Connor sang about "twisting a little closer," he loosened up by concentrating on the dark, faceless people in back. Meanwhile Eric and I did the backup bits and managed to smile at each other. Jon was the cool professional with the drum-stick twist. The stage lights dusted us red and green, making us look like real rock stars. We were jammin'.

The vocals were slightly off-key, the chord changes were a little sloppy, and the drums had a tendency to climb on top of everything, but somehow we added up to more than the sum of our inadequate parts. We let go of the fear and willed ourselves into being. We were a team, a unit, a band—and Mary was down front gazing up in full veneration.

At the end of the song, when the part came for us to each take a note and do the *ahh, ahhh, ahhhh, ahhhhhh* thing, I got a glimmer of what it must have been like for the real Beatles as they played for the huge crowd at Shea Stadium back in 1964.

It didn't last, though. The natives soon got restless. They stood around in bored clutches and impatient pairs, wondering what had happened to John Cougar, Fleetwood Mac, and REO Speedwagon.

"Play 'Eye of the Tiger,' dude!" some guy in a mack jacket finally shouted.

The smart-ass got a few laughs, but we ignored him for the enthusiastic cheers of Mary and her cohorts and a smattering of polite applause from the corners of the room. Then we nodded at one another in preparation for "A Hard Day's Night." I started it off with a punching strum, and Connor sang the anthem big and proud as if he'd written it himself.

We took the mob through "Sergeant Pepper's Lonely Hearts Club Band" and "Back in the U.S.S.R." To our relief the hecklers finally surrendered and decided to enjoy themselves. The pop purists in the crowd, those more interested in the Go-Gos or the J. Geils Band, sat around tables sipping spiked punch and being martyrs. Not one to mince words between songs, Connor ended each tune with "Th-th-thanks," no matter what we got in the way of positive reinforcement. Then, after "Revolution," Jon crashed out a big finish on the drums as the completely wet Connor gave the microphone cord one last whip. The lights went dim and we all gawked at one another in the settling dust of our first set in front of a live audience.

"We *rule*!" I cried, nearly floating off the stage toward Mary and her friends. They were all quivering, waiting to get close to the band.

Canned music came back on—Duran Duran's "Rio"—and the kids took to the floor. There were easily twice as many people dancing as when we were onstage, but we didn't care.

Mary brushed past the girls who were taking a closer look at the cute drummer. She walked right up to me, threw her arms around my neck, and kissed me. Everyone was watching.

"You were perfect," she declared.

"I don't think everyone likes the Beatles."

"*We* do."

Then, to our utter amazement, Todd emerged from the crowd and made his way toward the band. He was all smiles and full of pride. Attached to his arm was a homely female who constantly wiped dark, greasy hair out of her eyes, trying to arrange it behind her ears. It was a little too short for that sort of manoeuvre, and it ended up in her face again. She said nothing.

Todd shook our hands. "You guys weren't half bad."

Jon broke the awkward silence. "Thanks. Didn't expect you to be here."

"I'm not. And neither are you."

We were glad Todd had come but couldn't think of anything to say to him. He grinned and bobbed his head. Then Mary pulled me aside. Her cheeks were flushed, and I kissed them both. "Bill, I need to tell you something before you get the wrong idea."

"What's that, babe?"

"I...well..." She bit her bottom lip and shifted her weight from one leg to the other. "You're going to see me dancing a little with André."

André was her ex. He drove around in a blue-and-white Ford Bronco with wide tires—a sixteenth-birthday present from his life-insurance-selling father. I had seen him around town often enough. He always looked smug and self-satisfied. I wanted to slash his tires.

When André and Mary were together, he tried to push her too fast toward the naked stuff. Eventually he lost interest and bailed. I was convinced Mary had forgotten all about him since going out with me, since the equipment room.

"We're just going to dance a little and talk," she said. "That's all. We're only friends, but I didn't want you to get the wrong idea." She gave me a peck on the cheek.

"Wrong idea? I don't care who you dance with."

"But I thought that—"

"Well, don't think," I snapped. "Dance with whoever you want. It's your business."

"Bill, don't freak out."

"Do I sound like I'm freaking out?" I pointed at the stage. "I'm having the time of my life up there. You dancing with Andrew won't change that."

"*André.*"

"Whatever."

"I think you're taking this the wrong way."

"Mary, I gotta go."

Jon, Connor, and Eric pulled themselves away from Mary's eager friends. As the deejay took the stage, I saw Todd rush up to him and whisper something that made him smile.

"Are we havin' fun yet?" the deejay asked. Some of the kids indicated they might be. "I said, are we having fun yet?" Now a few more seemed convinced. "That's more like it!" He switched the mike from one hand to the other and worked the stage as if he were the main attraction.

"All right people. You know, there's a little mystery surrounding these guys and I've finally gotten to the bottom of it. First, I hear we all got the band's name wrong." He gestured to the banner above the stage. "And the other secret I'm gonna keep because, hey, they're good guys and they're playing their hearts out for us tonight. So let's at least give them a proper introduction. Ladies and gentlemen, boys and girls, members of the faculty and administration, please put your hands together for the Virgin Cure!"

There was a moment of silence, then wild cheering and applause. Eric tickled his bass, and Connor threw himself into "Day Tripper." Then, suddenly, it happened. We all arrived at a place where we let the song go. We watched it stretch its wings and come to life. I was home for the very first time. This was my destiny. I saw a blur of cities and arenas opening up before us, with fancy food on silver trays rolling into chic hotel rooms, and girls packed ten-deep pressing their breasts against our limo.

Then I saw Mary and André. Connor spotted them, too. He took a break from his stage strutting, worked his way back from the crowd, and gave me his what-the-hell expression, gesturing to what I had already seen. Mary and her ex were in the middle of the dance floor. We were halfway through "Day Tripper," not a slow song. Still, he was plastered against her, sliding his slimy hands down to her ass. I stopped playing, undid the guitar strap, and placed the instrument in the middle of the stage. As the song limped toward the finish line, I walked off the stage past the deejay, past Todd and his girlfriend with the bad hair, past Jon's growing fan club, past Mary and André. I never looked back.

✺

A lone light on a pole bathed the metal bleachers of the Ennis High football field in a sepia glow. I lit a cigarette and sent a jet of blue into the night as Connor and Eric stomped toward me like a couple of indignant parents.

"I just w-wanna know who you t-think you are." Connor bounced around in front of me, waving his arms in the air. "We were h-h-happenin' up there and p-p-people were sss-sss-ssstartin' to get into it and—"

"We were supposed to be in this thing together," Eric spat. "I had to grab your stupid guitar and try to make it through the rest of the set. I suck at guitar, and what's rock and roll without a bass? Don't *ever* do that again!" He shoved me and I quickly pushed him back. Jon showed up just in time to stop Eric from coming at me again.

I took a drag on my cigarette and snarled, "Yeah, well, fuck all of you!"

Jon stared at the grass, while the others boiled away in stunned silence.

"Aren't you going to dump on me, too?" I asked, glaring at Jon. "Don't you have something to add?"

Jon just shook his head and walked into the shadows, his hands shoved deep in his pockets. Then he was gone.

"Well, smart-ass," Eric yelled, "aside from ruining the entire gig, now we've got no place to stay tonight! I know this is going to be hard for you, *Bill*, but try thinking about other people for once in your life. Selfish prick." He turned to Connor. "You deal with him." Then he pounded off after Jon.

Connor's chest rose and fell as he worked up the nerve to speak again. He took a deep breath and opened his mouth, but nothing came out. Then he gave up.

"Mary was all over that stinking Adrian," I said.

"A-André."

"Whatever! God. I don't care who she dances with, but why does she have to throw it back in my face in front of everyone, in front of you guys? I was having a blast. We were cruisin'."

Connor looked away. He was back onstage, flirting with the audience.

"Man, I thought she loved me," I continued. "The way she was in the equipment room…"

Connor nodded.

"You know, I didn't give a shit at first. Really. I mean, I liked her and all, but I just wanted to… Well, you know how it is. You've had girls. At first I wanted her, and now I… Forget it." I flicked my cigarette butt into the field. "We rocked, didn't we?"

"Did you s-see the g-groupies?"

"They were after Jon. And you."

"It w-w-was cool. It w-was…real."

I lit another cigarette. "Did she leave with André?"

"No. They put on c-c-canned music. She w-w-was still d-dancin' to 'Eye of the Tiger.'" Then, as a consolation prize, he added, "The s-slut."

"Yeah. The slut. Figures."

SIXTEEN

NIGHT SWIMMING

Father Albert told us to "Go in peace to love and serve the Lord." After the monks performed their orderly retreat from the church, my associates and I filed out of our pew, genuflected, and started the march back to the dining hall for coffee. I hadn't even made it out of the church before I felt a clammy grip on the back of my neck. Slowly I turned to confirm that the hand was connected to the arm of Brother Thomas.

We walked like that past the rest of the student body. They all knew exactly what it meant. I was being cut from the herd in the calm, direct manner that signalled to everyone I was in trouble. The grip always came when I least expected it. It was confirmation I had been picking just a little too long the scab of Order and Decorum that was supposedly holding the whole place together.

It seemed strange that no one said anything. There was no reading of rights, no announcement that I was indeed being hauled in for questioning. No one even bothered to tell me what the charges

147

were. That was one of the more endearing traits of the seminary: so much was conveyed without words. One thing was certain, though. I wouldn't be eating breakfast.

✳

"No, William, I don't see an Orwellian conspiracy here." Brother Thomas had me cornered in the vacant science room. "It started when Father Gregory mentioned he saw Michael Ashbury sleeping in your bed."

"That little creep. What was he—"

"You made it back to Mass that morning, but you were late."

"I was in the bathroom. I wasn't feeling—"

"I thought it was a little strange at first, so I asked around and found out that Jon, Eric, and Connor all had excuses for being away that same Friday night. When Connor came back—wisdom teeth still firmly anchored in his skull—I got a little suspicious."

"He got bumped."

"So I called his parents. They weren't impressed."

I decided he must be interrogating us separately, hoping one of us would sing.

"The abbey has many friends in Ennis," he continued. "We have a pretty good idea what goes on down there. We received several calls. They all reported that the four of you were seen *performing* at a dance. Next time try asking for permission instead of forgiveness."

"Father Gregory, our *rector*, would have said no. *You* just wouldn't understand."

"It's you, my friend, who is operating under a gross misconception."

"Brother, I'm sorry. I really do wish I'd asked you."

"Don't patronize me, William. I didn't bother calling the other boys in. I know you got this whole thing off the ground. They're merely accomplices."

Presumed guilt was a pillar of the seminary justice system.

"I wish you'd grow out of this irritating stage you seem to be going through. We'd *hoped* that as a scholarship student you'd be a little more respectful of what we're trying to accomplish here. For some reason your friends look up to you. It would be a shame to have to..." It looked as if he was going to say *suspend* or *expel*, but at Saint John the Divine those words were weapons pulled out only when there was the intent to use them.

"I'm not a gambling man," he said. "I play things pretty straight. But right now I have no choice but to take a risk on you." He took a deep breath and scratched the back of his head. "Believe it or not, we have something more important than your immaturity to deal with. We're in the unfortunate position of needing your help."

"Sure, Brother, what can I do?" The door of escape cracked slightly, and I slipped my best foot forward.

"Well, this isn't easy..." He seemed tired and sullen. "I also called Jon's parents."

I held my breath.

"The Bennings had some bad news. Very bad news. A friend of Jon's has died, a close friend, and his parents are very upset."

"Who?"

"A boy named Travis Quigley. Apparently he was one of Jon's closest friends."

We had all heard of Travis. When Jon first came to Saint John's, all of his stories were peppered with "Then Travis and I..." and "My friend Travis says..." and so on. I'd never met him.

"Mrs. Benning asked for you to call her. She wanted to speak with you specifically. Jon doesn't know yet." He smoothed the wrinkles in his habit. "I'm not sure why she doesn't tell him herself. She must have her reasons. She's decided to entrust this duty to you. I hope you're up to it."

He fished around in the hidden pockets of his habit for a slip of paper, then pushed it across the desk to me. It had Jon's number on it. It said: "Call collect."

※

The junior French class had finished watching *Casablanca* dubbed in French. Father Albert abhorred traditional teaching methods and was forever lecturing us on the power of "progressive" education. Mostly these experiments consisted of trying new gimmicks to enliven his classes. The result was that we really didn't learn much, especially French, but saw some great movies and had a ball.

"Well, boys, what did you think of that one?" he asked, pushing the rewind button with a flourish. "Bogart was *très bien, non?*"

"*Oui, Père,*" we chanted.

In our sophomore year all the instructions in Brother Stephen's French class were in French. Father Albert couldn't be bothered.

"You know, this is one of my favourite movies of all time." He wandered over to the window and peered at the Bog and Mount Saint John to clear his mind and sharpen his focus on the past. "I was too young for the war, of course. But let me tell you, I would've been the first to sign up if I'd been a few years older."

"*Bien sûr, Père,*" we chimed in unison.

He looked at us out of the corner of his eye to make sure we weren't mocking him. In particular he glared at Dean, then turned back toward the window. "Of course, if I *had* served during the war, I might have been posted in the European Theatre, working to destabilize Vichy and liberate France, mightn't I, Dean?"

"*Oui, c'est possible.*"

"Tell us about the French Resistance, Dean. Anything."

Fact was, Father Albert hated teaching French because he didn't have a good command of the language. He loved Latin and made sure everyone knew he was teaching this "inferior" language under duress. We all had our little crosses to bear, and he made it plain this was his. He did, however, like movies, World War II, and classical music. To make it easier on all of us, we tried working these subjects into our dialogues whenever possible.

In his best Level II French, Dean said, more or less, "What I know of the formidable French Resistance I studied from the excellent film *Casablanca.*"

Dean continued to tell us of Rick's Café Américain, Humphrey Bogart and Ingrid Bergman's romance, and dirty Nazi collaborators. He knew many of those wonderful lines long before ever seeing the film. *Nous avons Paris toujours.* This got a big smile from Father

Albert. He finished by saying that the way he remembered most of his French vocabulary was from watching American movies dubbed in French. He concluded by saying, "It is a fun way to learn."

"*Très bien*, Dean. You flatter me, but that's allowed." Father Albert glanced at his watch. "All right, gentlemen, you know your homework. Do it. And if you have any questions, consult your French-English dictionary or one of your more learned classmates. For next Monday's and Wednesday's classes we're going to watch *The Bridge on the River Kwai* and discuss Japanese imperialism." He turned and put the videotape into its case. No one ever bothered asking what the hell any of this had to do with French. The bell went off, binders slapped shut, and everyone shuffled out of the room.

I had been staring at the back of Jon's head the entire class, dreading what I was about to do. He was on his way to music class, and I waited until he was halfway down the hall before overtaking him. "Hey, Jon, let's go for a walk. We have to talk."

"We've got music class."

"I know. Let's skip it today."

"Let's not."

"Jon…" I grabbed his arm for emphasis. "It's important. We're gonna skip today." He searched my expression for a hint of the trouble, then followed me out the front door and down the drive.

It was a gorgeous day, sunny and bright, big leaves of rust, pumpkin, and gold rustling in the trees and lying about in silent drifts. It was one of those days that made you wonder what you ever saw in summer.

We stopped at the butternut tree near the gym and sat on a clear spot in the dewy grass. Jon studied me, then looked away. "If this has anything to do with what we were talking about a few weeks ago…"

"It doesn't. I just got off the phone with your mother this morning."

He paused for a moment, not knowing how to proceed. "Yeah?"

"She says you haven't been getting along with either of them for the past couple of months, so she wanted to speak with me. She figured—"

"They have no right trying to get you on their side. God, they piss me off."

"Listen, man, this has nothing to do with you and them. This is about your friend Travis. He's..." My throat constricted. I wasn't ready to tell him, and he would never be ready to hear it. I had prepared a speech, but it seemed silly now. He was impatient for the truth. I stared into his vulnerable brown eyes and braced myself before hurting him again. "He's dead."

"What?"

"He drowned, man. I'm sorry."

Jon blinked a few times, then said, "He's a good swimmer."

"They think he did it on purpose."

"Impossible!"

"Oh, man, it's true. They think he meant to." I couldn't make myself say *suicide*.

Jon got up and took a few tentative steps toward the drive, his backside wet from the grass. He clasped his hands over his head. "Shit."

"Your folks want you to call them as soon as you're ready. There's going to be a funeral in a couple of—" Jon was already running down the drive, tie and blazer flapping at his back. I gave him a head start, then stood and checked my pants. They, too, were wet. Slowly I walked to the back of the gym and picked up Connor's bike, tucked my pant leg into my sock, and coasted downhill in search of Jon.

When I caught up to him about a half mile down the road to Ennis, he was walking with his head bowed. He didn't acknowledge me and kept on going. I jumped off the bike and strolled beside him. "He sounded like an excellent guy," I said, feeling dumb.

"He was."

"When was the last time you saw him?"

"Just before I left for the seminary. He was pissed at me. He was jealous that I got to go away to school and he didn't. He hated public school." Jon stopped and faced me. "Can I ask you something? Why are you chasing me and everything? I mean, I know my mom's too weak to deal with reality, but this isn't your problem."

"What do you mean? You're my friend and this is heavy shit. I want to talk to you."

"Best friend. You used to say I was your *best* friend." Silent tears spilled down his cheeks, the kind he'd shed back in the chapel the other day. "You didn't want to talk before."

"Hey, wait a minute," I said. "This is *different*."

"No, it's not. You're supposed to listen to your friends when they need it, not just when you're in the fucking mood for it or someone else asked you to."

I wanted to defend myself, to show him I wasn't the jerk he was making me out to be, but my voice had deserted me.

Jon brushed the hair back off his forehead, reminding me of my father, and then rubbed his face. "Why don't you go back up? I'll be fine. I'm just going to take a walk. I'll be back when I'm ready." A car whisked by, kicking up little bits of gravel and leaves.

"Jon, you should talk this thing through."

"Leave me alone," he whispered, moving away from me.

I pushed the bike off the road, then ran ahead of Jon and blocked his path. When he tried to step past, I threw my arms around him. He tried to push me away, but I held him close. I could feel his muscles relax as his head slumped on my shoulder. For a few minutes, as I held him, he sobbed quietly, wetting my shirt through to the skin.

A pickup truck drove by with two men. They looked out the back window with angry faces. The brake lights flashed as the truck slowed down and pulled onto the shoulder. I loosened my grip on Jon.

"I told you to fuck off," he suddenly growled, shoving me away. "I want to be by myself."

Jon continued down the road toward Ennis, wiping his face and kicking rocks out of the way. Finally the driver of the truck lost interest in us, found first gear, and drove off. I was completely alone, standing there with Connor's old bike and a chill deep inside.

SEVENTEEN

CONTAGION

The door, the crucifix over the door, and the wooden chairs separating each of the six beds were pretty much the only things that weren't white. The bed linen, walls, floor, medical cabinet, and pale, sick faces were all bleached of colour. The sole purpose of this room was to contain the Contagion.

We were booked into the infirmary with a stomach flu that had been chalking up casualties all over the seminary. Connor sat propped in his bed with a stack of pillows behind him, flipping through an old issue of *Sports Illustrated*. I lay flat on my back in the bed next to him with a T-shirt over my face, pretending to be someplace else. Helmut was tucked in there with us.

Father Gregory walked in and quickly closed the door behind him. "There were three hundred people at the funeral for Jon's friend. Anglican. Anyway, he'll be back on Monday, William. I want you and Connor to keep an eye on him. The community should rally around at a time like this."

"Sure, Father," Connor said.

Helmut had shiny blond hair that almost looked fake, like the kind put on dolls. All legs and arms, he was a natural-born goalie. If he really was sick, he didn't look it. To us, it seemed as if was taking a well-deserved break from the big routine. As usual Helmut kept to himself, pretending to read and not listening to what was being said. Father Gregory walked over to him and politely scooped up his novel for inspection. Espionage. Satisfied, he gave it back. "How are you feeling?"

"Better, Father. I think I'm ready to go back downstairs now."

"No, you're not. Stay the night and you can come back down in the morning."

"All right, Father," Helmut said meekly. "If you say so."

I responded with a barely audible sucking sound.

"What's that?" As Father Gregory spun around, his shoes squeaked. "Stay out of trouble, William. Connor, I'm holding you responsible for anything he does."

"W-what? I'm n-not my brother's k-keeper. He's not even—"

"Just try to act like adults. And don't leave the infirmary. You'll spread the Contagion." Father Gregory came over to my bed and pulled the T-shirt off my face. "I'm expecting a lot from you when Jon arrives. You stick with him. Understand?"

"Sure, Father."

"Oh, and a friend of yours called. Mary O'Brien. I told her you weren't feeling well and that personal calls are reserved for Saturdays and Sundays only. Take care, boys." His habit swished as he turned, stepped out into the hall, and quickly sealed the door behind him.

It wasn't fair. On the outside kids could call in sick and play hooky all day. Or, if they really were sick, stay home and watch TV on the couch. When you complained of something at Saint John's, you were quarantined. With no distractions, you were left to concentrate on getting better. That meant you avoided getting sick at all costs.

"At least in jail they have TVs," I said. "This place is like one of those Commie insane asylums where they put political prisoners. They want to break our spirits."

"William, " Connor said, "s-shut up."

"What do you say, Mutt?" I asked. Most everyone called Helmut Mutt. I would have hated being called that. "This joint remind you of those loony bins in East Berlin?"

"I was born in West Germany."

"Are you sure you're not a spy—one of those deep-cover sleeper agents who gets settled in a quiet little town, then breaks out when the Kremlin gives the order?"

"Very funny."

Helmut's family had moved from Munich to Canada when he was a little kid. His mother was German and his dad was a Canadian air force officer. He had been educated on base and didn't have a trace of an accent. But that name!

Just then Michael Ashbury pushed open the door with a bright green tray of food. I sat up. Confused and a little afraid, he set the tray down on the medicine cabinet. A deep-fried odour caught up to him and filled the room. That, combined with the fact that I hadn't been vertical in a long time, sent blood rushing to my head, nauseating me slightly.

"What is it?" I finally asked.

Michael Ashbury held his breath, trying hard not to contract the Contagion. "Fish sticks," he whispered, letting out as little air as possible. "It's Friday."

✳

I had thrown up twice since entering the infirmary but was feeling much improved. Connor had puked after tasting the Friday fish sticks but was still riding that just-purged euphoria. Forty-eight hours in the cooker encouraged us to find signs of rapid improvement in our physiological state and gave us an insatiable need to seek out some form of entertainment/danger. But first we had to change out of our pajamas. Around midnight we slipped past the sleeping Helmut and out the infirmary door.

We reconnoitered the hall for signs of the enemy. Finding none, we headed straight for Jon's wardrobe and the removable board under which he had hidden the key to the attic. It was all just a little *too* easy. We encountered no opposition during the first leg of the operation, except for Eric. While he was still sleeping, Connor pinned him as I put my hand over his mouth to preempt any outburst that might jeopardize the mission. Gasping, he tried to sit up and made quite a scene before we were able to subdue him. Eric didn't want to come up with us for fear of getting caught, and then he whined at us for spreading germs all over him.

When Connor and I reached the attic, we tiptoed through it past the costumes and all the boxed files of secrets until we found ourselves at the ham-radio room and the frontier of the unknown. Beyond the weakening flashlight beam stretched two dark passages. One, we reasoned, must lead toward the church, the other toward the monks' rec room. Somehow we ended up over the kitchen, which wasn't such a bad thing. We removed a service panel over the oven and carefully climbed down into the shadows and stainless steel.

We had rediscovered our appetite, but Brother Ambrose's cookie tin was nowhere to be found. We rummaged through shelves, cupboards, and the walk-in cooler. Then we found it: a case of Vachon cakes.

"They keep these for themselves," I said. "Ever seen a Joe Louis within a mile of this place?"

"Never."

"Well, then, under this monastic Communist-regime I say we have a right to our fair share."

"Fucking-A."

We sat on the floor and ploughed into the chocolate hockey pucks. I was into my third when the secret slipped out, like a joke or a comment about the weather.

"Jon's a homo," I announced. "I grabbed his binder by accident. It had the photo of Tom's dink and a picture of a naked statue. There was nothing he could say."

"Are you s-s-sure?"

"Positive. You think you know a guy and then—shit, it's so weird."

"So you th-think he's a t-tail gunner?"

"Yeah…I don't know. Maybe he's just confused or something. It kinda makes you go back and think about everything he's said and done. You never expect someone close to you to…"

Connor eyed the box of Wagon Wheels and considered taking a fourth. He changed his mind and leaned his head against a shelf holding giant cans of tomatoes.

"Jon's mom thinks his friend committed suicide," I continued. "But she didn't give any details."

"You th-think this T-Travis guy was…sorta in on it with Jon?"

I shrugged. "When I think about it, it makes me mad."

"What do you m-mean?"

"It's not right. He's been lying to us all these years. We're in here together, stuck like sardines. He broke a trust. A *sacred* trust."

Connor considered what I'd said.

"It's like he's been one of us all this time, then *bam!* He's not what he seems to be. Think about it. How are we ever going to feel safe again?" I paused for effect. "I'm sorry for him, but I still can't help the way I feel."

"You're his best friend. Has he ever…you know, t-tried anything on you?"

"Of course not. But he's probably thinking about it." My betrayal was complete.

"He gave you his w-watch. What's t-t-that all about?"

"When you're friends with someone, you should be able to take a few things for granted. Like the fact he's not thinking about you when he jerks off."

"Geez, Bill, d-don't g-gross me out."

My stomach churned. "You're my best friend. I just thought you should know about Jon." The room began to tilt. As I rose to escape, the Joe Louises welled up in a big, hot wave, and I barely made it to the sink.

⚚

When Jon returned that Saturday night, he looked considerably older. He didn't have much to say, especially to me. I was lounging on my bed when he came upstairs to dump his stuff into his wardrobe. He kept his coat and scarf on and said he was glad to be back, but he wouldn't even look at me.

That night I tried to get a band practice together, but Jon wasn't interested and Connor was "too busy." Eric and I played a few tunes in the rec room and talked about how great we'd been at the Oktoberfest dance. We told each other that was the way all great bands started out and, hey, you never knew, we just might get discovered.

❋

The political stability of the seminary was rapidly deteriorating. The rumours and signs of insurrection were everywhere. Father Gregory finally figured out that Todd was a megalomaniac when he caught him dumping a huge pile of crumbs, dust, and garbage on the bed of a grade eighter. The kid had postponed sweeping the dining-hall floor one afternoon because of a special piano lesson Father Albert had arranged with one of the guests. Although Father Gregory took Todd aside and had words with him, this had little positive effect. The student body completely shunned the Senior Senior now. In effect, he no longer existed. We were in our dorm stripping our beds when we heard his voice.

"Just what the hell do you think you're doing?" Todd was confronting Michael Ashbury out in the hall at the Sunday Morning Sheet Exchange.

"Nothing." Michael was separating and bagging bed linen with his goalie stick. He wore his Boston Bruins jersey, goalie's mask, and gloves.

"Nothin'? Then what's this getup for?"

"I don't wanna catch nothin' from the sheets," Michael whined. "Some guys are peeing in their beds and, *you know*, if I touch 'em I might get lice or VD."

While few of us ever actually had sex, there was the perceived possibility of catching the clap or something worse by drinking from the same cup, sitting on the same toilet seat, or even touching dirty sheets. At Saint John the Divine *sex* and *education* were mutually exclusive terms.

Connor, Eric, Jon, and I were crowded at the door, watching

the action. Tom Wolosovic came by with his hair sticking up and his shirt half tucked in. Oblivious to the standoff, he dropped his dirty stuff on the floor, picked up his new sheets, and headed back to the nursery. As Todd looked on, Michael gingerly nudged the pillowcase away from the sheets with the hockey stick, scooted it into its own pile, then pulled the fitted sheet away from the flat sheet and put them into separate piles. He was careful not to let even his glove touch the potential Contagion.

"Now I've seen it all," Todd said. "No one here has any diseases, and you're not going to spread stupid rumours."

"I'm not spreading rumours."

"Take off the gloves," Todd ordered.

"No."

"Do it or you're dead."

"Leave me alone. I'm not hurting anybody."

Todd grabbed the stick from Michael and tossed it onto the floor. He tugged the gloves off his hands, pulled the mask off his head, then turned him around and pushed him face-first into the pile of dirty fitted sheets.

Michael got up as fast as possible and wiped himself of the unseen Contagion. His face was flushed and a vein throbbed in his neck. "We've *had* it with you, Todd! You'd better watch out!"

"What's that supposed to mean, punk?"

Jon moved forward. "Leave him alone. He's just doing his job. Go pick on somebody else."

Todd sneered at John, then turned again to Michael. "I'm writing you up for that little outburst and the shitty job you're doing."

Jon marched back into our dorm. A second later he returned with his dirty sheets. He stared straight up at Todd and then, with great ceremony, dumped the sheets in a pile at Michael's feet. Bending down, he picked up the hockey stick and put it back into Michael's hand. Michael got the rest of his official National Hockey League armour off the floor, suited up, and defiantly stick-handled his way through the job. As for Todd, he stomped down the hall, shaking his head and muttering to the world at large and at no one in particular.

EIGHTEEN

THE DYING ROOM

The Student Council meeting was a showcase of petty strife. The name implied some sort of control over our own affairs, which was, of course, impossible. Convened at the beginning, middle, and end of each semester, these gatherings were actually designed to identify and contain any potential threats to the state of Good Order. They offered an opportunity for Father Gregory to put his bony old finger to the pulse of the student body. Everyone was in the rec room. Everyone was a member of the Student Council. We were discussing financial matters when I finally started paying attention.

"If we only have enough money for one, I say it makes more sense to keep *Time*," Eric said. "That's about the only way we can find out what's going on in the real world."

Hands were raised. Father Gregory and Dean, seated behind a table onstage, were moderating the debate. Dean scanned the crowd, then nodded to Connor. "The chair recognizes Connor."

Connor stood and straightened his shirt. He was actually going to speak in public. "I...well, s-s-some of us w-w-wanna k-k-keep s-subscribing to *Sports Illustrated*." He sat down, panting as if he'd just run up a flight of stairs. Cheers went up around the room.

A smile curled across Eric's face as he rose. "Mr. Chairman?"

"The council recognizes Eric."

"We already get the sports section of the newspaper," he said with feigned patience. "*Sports Illustrated* only covers sports. *Time* covers everything. International news, features, music, entertainment, *and* sports."

Todd glanced over his shoulder and said, "Eric, give it up."

"Order *please*," Father Gregory moaned.

Connor and Eric couldn't look at each other. The debate had been raging for twenty minutes, mostly with Eric's impassioned advertisements for *Time*. It was, of course, the principle. Someone had to win and someone had to lose. At Saint John the Divine the principle often gained in significance as the issues diminished in size.

Helmut stood. "Eric may be right, but more of us are interested in sports and couldn't care less about all that other stuff. I vote for *SI*."

Eric raised his hand, then jumped up. "For *some* people there's more to life than football scores. I mean, aren't we supposed to be getting an education here? And if we're not allowed to watch TV, then how else are we supposed to keep up with current events and politics and international stuff?"

"Read the paper!" someone shouted from the back of the room.

Eric peered down at me for support, his eyes sharp and determined. I shrugged, playing Switzerland on this one and loving it.

People began to murmur.

"Eric still has the floor," Dean said.

"Then I think we should vote on it," Eric said. "Anyone second the motion?"

Connor punched the air above his head.

Dean, seemingly weary of it all, leaned across the table on his elbows. "All right, all in favour of *Time*..." About a third raised timid hands. "*Sports Illustrated?*" Everyone else saluted. I abstained. "*SI* it is."

Eric shot a sour look past me to Connor, who gave him his Nixon victory salute and hissed, *"Yessssss!"* Eric's face reddened, as if he'd been sitting too close to a fire.

"All right, people, any other business?" Dean yelled above the din.

Michael Ashbury raised his hand. "I want to hold a meeting of all the underclassmen after this." People got quiet for him. "Out in the gym. Underclassmen. No one else."

Father Gregory looked puzzled for a moment, then yawned.

"That's it," Dean announced. "This meeting is adjourned."

"One more item if I may, Mr. Chairman." Brother Thomas, who must have slipped in unnoticed halfway through the meeting, now strode to the stage and turned to face the assembly. He wore his stock "gravely disappointed" look, only this time it was worse.

"The chair recognizes Brother Thomas."

"Thank you. It has come to our attention that a serious breach of trust has taken place at Saint John's. There's been a break-and-enter in the monastery."

Confusion spread like spilled gas. Not the Satanists again!

"A room in the attic above the monks' cells has been broken into and searched."

Suddenly the blood left my brain and headed south for my Hush Puppies. I didn't dare glance at Connor or Eric, but the energy emanating from them was enough to roast a pig.

"We're not sure when it happened, but someone, or a group of someones, broke into the room and disturbed some very sensitive equipment. He sat on the edge of the stage. "Now we don't have much to go on, but we're convinced this time it was an inside job."

My tongue stuck to the roof of my mouth. Connor brushed imaginary lint off his pants, and Jon was frozen, like a grouse trying to avoid detection.

"I feel it's important to remind the group that anyone violating the cloister is breaking one of this seminary's most important rules, not to mention Church Law," Brother Thomas announced. "The Holy Father, Pope—well, one of them, anyway, issued a decree on the sanctity of the cloister stating that those found willfully violating such an area can be *excommunicated*." He relished every syllable of the last word.

The room got unnaturally quiet, and Connor tried to cover his smile.

"I'm telling you this to illustrate the gravity of the situation. I'm going to leave it to you, gentlemen. By six o'clock tomorrow night, I expect the guilty person or persons to present themselves to one of the monks. This kind of thing won't be tolerated."

Obviously it was the first time Father Gregory had heard the news. We were excused, and they turned to each other to confer about the crime. As the student body dispersed into the seminary, Connor led us downstairs through the change room, past the showers, and into the drying room.

The warm cinder-block cell, narrow and two stories high, was filled with a spiderweb of clotheslines and countless shorts, jerseys, and socks—all caked with mud and sweat. A dirty wooden bench covered a heating pipe that bent around all four walls. It was a stuffy, reeking bunker. No one would follow us here.

The drying room had another name, not often heard. On a spring morning in 1963 a seminarian went missing. When the monks finally noticed he was gone, they called the cops and began a search that led them through Saint John the Divine and all over town. They even looked in here but found nothing. Three days passed. By that time they merely had to follow their noses. When they checked the second time, they looked up. Sure enough, the kid was hanging there, surrounded by dirty laundry, a rope cinched tightly around his neck. He left a short note, but no one really knew why he had done it. Even though almost twenty years had passed, now and then someone would refer to the place as the Dying Room. If a monk was within earshot, the idiot got slapped.

"Okay, we're in deep s-shit now," Connor whispered to smooth his stutter. "Jon, go g-get Eric. He needs to be in on t-this."

Jon left the room.

"We're dead," I announced, moving the ladder to make more room. "We're going to get found out, we're going to get ratted on, and we're going to get expelled. We're *dead*!"

"No, we're n-n-not."

"Yes, we are."

"William, r-relax."

"We've gotta figure this out," I said. "They can excommunicate all they want, but I'm not going home."

Eric and Jon squeezed in. "Brother Thomas is *pissed*!" Eric said, shutting the door behind them.

Jon kicked some cleats off the bench. "All the anklebiters are out in the gym. They're up to something."

"Who c-cares?" Connor whispered. "L-listen…"

Connor poured out his plan for transforming us into angels. We were to cease all illegal activities: no trips to the attic, no skipping study hall, and no more girls on campus. We had to keep our heads down and avoid any undue attention.

"And we have to stick together," I added. Everyone nodded. "I mean, *really* stick together." More nods. "We've got to protect each other. Loyalty is the only thing that's going to see us through this. It's just like when someone starts hitting on one of us, you know, picking a fight." Puzzlement. "Like the time those Baptists started that fight at the soccer game. We all had to cover each other's butt. It's the only way." I stared straight at Jon. "No one can stand on the sidelines this time."

Jon folded his arms across his chest. "What the hell are you trying to say, MacAvoy?"

"Just what I said."

"Are you saying I won't fight for my friends?"

"Take a pill," I snapped. "Don't be so sensitive."

"Well, if you're talking about that fight with the Baptists, that was *your* fault. You were riding that guy. You hacked him every chance you got. *That's* why I didn't jump in to save your ass. You deserved it."

Connor and Eric were shocked. Their eyes shifted back and forth between us as if they were watching a tennis match.

"I didn't start anything," I said. "You stayed away to save your own neck."

"You were a prick. You were just mad 'cause you were playing badly. I'll back you up when you're not bringing it all on yourself."

167

"You're supposed to back up your friends no matter what. Period."

Jon got up to leave. "I'm out of this."

Connor grabbed his arm. "We got to s-s—"

Jon pulled his arm away. "Don't worry. I'm going to keep it a secret. Just don't bother me anymore." Jon slammed the door so hard the change in pressure nearly popped our ears.

Connor shook his head in disgust, then got up to leave. "W-what's wrong w-w-with you?"

"He was the one who got the attic key in the first place," I said.

Connor stared at me as if he were decoding the words, as if I were speaking Level III Latin. "I guess y-you two r-really are div-v-vorced."

I hated him in that instant. Every muscle in my body tensed, then I lunged and shoved him into the wall as hard as I could. Connor easily righted himself and whispered, "You really want to take me on?" I stood there with my arms at my side, unable to move.

He shook his head, turned, and walked out, taking Eric with him. The door slammed shut and I sat alone, peering into the drain in the floor and breathing in the stench of the student body.

✻

It took forever to fall asleep. I played the same image over and over again in my mind. The scene was always my funeral. Who would show up? Who would miss me? I pictured my dad, upset but relieved that I was going to take his dirty little secret to the grave with me. My brother and sisters, remembering the cute little brat they knew before leaving home for college, would probably cry because it seemed the right thing to do. Would any of my old friends from public school show up? Would Connor, Eric, or Mary bother making the trek to Calgary? Would Jon feel the hole inside, like the one I was feeling now? Three hundred people for Travis… Only my mother would cry for me.

All this had one positive effect. My prayers had finally been answered. I had lost the urge to abuse myself. And still I prayed and prayed. In Latin, French, and English. I called out to Jesus, Mary, and Saint Jude to help me make things right. But only darkness and silence came back as the candle of faith snuffed out.

Why didn't I feel God's presence anymore? Where was His healing light? In my heart I shouted His name, but the echo just went on and on. I was orphaned, abandoned. In the place of that sweet dependence grew something else, something terrible and absolute—the realization that I was completely alone. There was nowhere else to look for solace, nowhere else to put the blame.

I slept without covers to make myself uncomfortably cold. When everyone else was asleep, I lay down next to my bed on the hard terrazzo floor. No covers or pillow. I stared at Jon's shoes sticking out from under his bed. I curled up like a baby, shivered, and offered up a final, desperate prayer: *Ave Maria, gratcia plena, Dominus tecum...*

A little later I awoke in the dark to see Father Gregory standing over me, nudging my ribs with the toe of one of his silent slippers. I looked up, and although he was well camouflaged for night, I saw him rub an eye with one hand and his rosary beads with the other. He paused in his prayers long enough to whisper, "You fell out of bed. Get back in."

✳

The rain had been coming down without a break all day. It was Sunday, and no one was going to town. The last time I had visited Saint Theresa's, Mr. Thorpe was gone. He still wasn't dead, but he couldn't talk or recognize people or use his hands very well. Apparently there wasn't much going on in his head anymore, so he had been shipped home to his daughter to finish out his diminished life with her. I couldn't help wondering why she hadn't wanted him when he was still lucid.

I grabbed Connor's big red poncho, put on my rubber boots, and headed out into the cold and grey. I wandered past the bell tower and the church, through the woods, and into the orchard where well-ordered rows of hazelnut, plum, and apricot trees marched down the hill into the pasture. The fruit trees were bare, but the hazelnuts retained a wet-brown canopy. Last year's leaves still hung on in the hope that if things didn't get worse, they might just make it through winter.

The rain made loud, obnoxious splats against the poncho's hood, and time moved like old Father Ezekiel: steadily, carefully, rationing effort. I passed the Bog, rippled with a billion tiny raindrops, and the statue of Our Lady of the Lake. I had never felt this way before—utterly alone. I thought about giving Mary a call.

As I strode across the slick stones of the Appian Way, I heard the anklebiters in the gym. They were playing a frantic game of basketball, shoving and fouling under a net where the old crucifix used to hang, running up and down the open court once blocked with a rigid row of pews.

Helmut sat at the top of the bleachers reading a comic book. Jon slouched at the bottom, watching the Shirts battle the Skins. I shook off the rain and hung the poncho on a hook near the door, then ambled over and sat beside Jon.

Michael Ashbury was at the top of his form. Short but fast, he darted and dodged through the bigger players with confidence, passing and shooting the Skins to victory. As I sat on the sidelines, I realized I had watched Michael change during this unending semester. Just as he was beginning his rise, I was in free fall—with no end in sight.

"You know, I—"

"I don't want to hear it," Jon told me. We listened instead to the chirp of rubber soles on the varnished oak floor. "You told me how you feel."

"I missed you."

Michael had the ball again and was looking to make a pass. The options weren't attractive, so he made a break, spun around his man, and took a shot. At the last second someone jumped up and tipped it out of the way.

"Travis didn't kill himself," Jon said. "My mom doesn't always get the details before she talks. She watches too much *Donahue*."

"What?"

"He was drinking and fell off a boat. They didn't even notice for a long time. It was dark. He was too drunk to swim. End of story."

"Then how come your mom said—"

"She just...you know. They jump to conclusions. I guess there've been a lot of teenage suicides in West Vancouver." He looked as if he was about to turn and face me, but he didn't. "I'm sorry about the fight at the soccer game. You were right. I should have backed you up."

"I'm the one who should apologize."

"And let's set the record straight. Travis had nothing to do with...what I tried to tell you back in the chapel. He didn't even know about me. No one knew except you."

"Like I said, let's forget all that."

"Then why did you tell Connor? Are you out to get me because I didn't fight the Baptists for you, or is it something else?"

Suddenly there wasn't enough oxygen to go around. "I...I didn't tell!"

Jon finally looked my way. His eyes were cold and angry. "Maybe you're right, Bill. Maybe I'm just a bit screwed up. But what I don't understand is your telling other people about..."

There was no use denying it. "I needed to get some...*advice*. It's not like I told just anyone. I told Connor. We're your friends."

"I hope Connor is better at it than you are. I don't think I could handle two *friends* like you. And where's all this 'sticking together' bullshit you were preaching about? I didn't want Connor to know. I trusted you. With everything."

I felt like swallowing my tongue.

"At first I thought God was punishing me," he continued, turning back to the game. "No matter how hard I tried I couldn't stop thinking about it. I couldn't stop thinking about you."

Someone scored on a long shot. The Skins went wild and the Shirts regrouped.

"Then it dawned on me. God isn't punishing me. He's just showing me I'm strong enough to make it on my own."

"Jon—"

"I didn't need you to feel the same way about me. I just needed you to be my friend. Now I don't need anybody."

He got up and walked across the vacant half of the court, heading for the door. Before he left the gym he turned toward me, tall and confident. I knew this was goodbye, not a mean or vindictive or even sad one, just goodbye, final and complete. When the door closed behind him, all I could hear was the basketball pounding in my ears.

NINETEEN

ELEMENTS OF SURPRISE

Sometimes I thought my mother had extrasensory perception, but it never seemed to do us any good. Her call came while I was folding clothes in the laundry room. I had never folded anything until I had come to Saint John the Divine. Nor had I ever washed my own underwear or known how difficult it was to get grass stains out of pants. As for soaking things overnight or separating colours from whites, forget it. I suppose every seminarian had particular, private moments when they thought of their mothers and mourned the fraying apron strings. Mine came each time I tucked one greying sock into its mate, forming one of my mother's perfect sock bundles.

Dean answered the phone. He told Jon to go downstairs and get me. Jon saw Connor and passed the message on to him. But Connor was on his way to take a leak. When he was done, he sauntered down into the bowels of the seminary to let me know my mother was on the line and that we were having a band practice later that afternoon. By the time I got to the phone, my mother had been listening to kids play grab-ass in the hall for six long-distance minutes.

"I'm fine," I told her.

"You don't sound fine to me."

"Well, I am."

She told me about her troubles with her boss, my brother, and my dad. I was the only man in her life who wasn't causing her grief. There were some big changes coming down the pike. She had her hands full and was at the end of her rope. She wanted to know what I thought she should do. I didn't know, and she didn't even know the half of it. Staying silent, I soaked up the sound of her voice.

"What's wrong, honey?"

"Nothing," I said. "I told you. I'm fine."

"I had a feeling I should call." She waited me out, adding another five or ten seconds of dead air to the phone bill.

"No one here likes me anymore."

"Sure they do, honey. You're just having a bad day."

She started up again about the other girls smoking in the salon, the cheap customers, my dad's sudden need for independence. I remembered the sound of the old clothes dryer at home, and a little boy who cuddled up against the warm vibration as his mother folded the laundry.

She had to go. The phone call was costing a fortune, and she had to get ready for work. I wondered why it was only phone calls that cost a fortune. Gas, food, rent—everything else was merely expensive.

✲

The crew was rounded up by Connor for a band practice in the rec room. We set up onstage without talking. Three freshmen were playing pool in the back corner. They ignored us as we tuned our instruments.

Connor had been humming "With a Little Help from My Friends" all day and thought it would be great if we played that. No one was interested. We decided on "Let It Be." It was the first time we tried playing it as a band. We kicked around different parts of the song, working on chord changes, fighting about how slow or fast it should be. When we finally got it off the ground, it picked up an angry, punkish momentum as Connor rasped about "Mother Mary" and "times of trouble."

Anklebiters began arriving singly and in groups. Taking no notice of us, they quietly searched out hiding places in the dust beneath the pool table, under stacks of metal chairs, behind the stage curtains or the door leading to the change rooms—anywhere capable of hiding an adolescent body.

Connor got up from his stool and sauntered to the edge of the stage, trying to grab some attention. He bowed his head and belted the song out with all the drama he could muster. No one took any notice. As Connor sang about patience and wisdom and there being some sort of "answer," I drifted farther and farther away.

We had all joined in on the chorus when Michael Ashbury raced down the stairs. The double doors crashed into the wall as he ran straight into the middle of the room and stopped. The boys at the pool table gazed up from their game with cool expectation. Then Todd stormed in, tight-jawed and fuming. He lunged at Michael. "You little asshole! I'm gonna tear your head off!"

Michael ducked, sidestepped, and cried, *"Go!"*

Although what happened next occurred in the blink of an eye, it threw our world into slow motion. The underclassmen mobilized from their camouflaged positions. From under and around the pool table, from under the stage and out of the storage locker, they came. The room burst at the seams with rabid thirteen- and fourteen-year-olds, swarming like frenzied ants. They attacked as a unit, kicking, punching, biting. Reinforcements came from upstairs until there were nearly twenty in the attack party. With ease they over-whelmed the Senior Senior and brought him down.

We stood quietly onstage, gripping our instruments like shields, watching the anklebiters extract their retribution. I saw bits of ripped shirt fly from the mob. I saw kids kick and punch so hard they exhausted themselves. I saw sweet satisfaction on faces that all became strangely similar. After several seconds of this unreality, Michael made it out of the pile and jumped on Todd's butt, yelling "Yes!" and "Feel this!" and "Don't fuck with us!"

Only moments before they had been insignificant, weak individuals, but they had transformed themselves into something powerful and dangerous. They had become a single being.

Then, as suddenly as the assault had begun, the swarm pulled back in a defensive circle, leaving Todd exposed on the floor. He struggled to his feet, revealing a bloody nose and lip, torn shirt and pants, and underwear pulled up to his ribs. A little blood even oozed from the side of his head where hair had been ripped away. His face was red and ashen. He took wild swings, but the mob maintained an even circle, taunting him from every side. The Senior Senior spat blood on a few of them, mumbling some unintelligible poison. Then Michael, coming down from the shot of adrenaline, said, "Okay, let him go."

Todd managed to slur, "You're all dead!" But it wasn't his voice. It was the voice of the little kid inside who had just been beaten beyond recognition. He gasped a little weirdly, rolled his head to one side, and passed out in a pile of defeat.

"He's dead! He's dead!" one of the smallest attackers proclaimed.

"No, he's not," someone else corrected. "He just fainted. Like a woman."

Towering over the Senior Senior, Michael spoke in a low, steady voice. "Try anything and you'll get it again." Then he stepped over the body and made his way to the door.

Michael Ashbury ascended the stairs, carried up more by pats on the back than any effort of his own. As the doors swung lazily behind the anklebiters, Jon jumped down to offer aid to Todd. The rest of us stared, mouths agape, marvelling at how the wheels of justice had spun out of control and run over Todd like a train.

Three rosaries later Connor, Eric, and I sat in the empty juniors' classroom, contemplating damage-control strategies. We loitered in the dark near the windows. The room was silent and still except for the soft clicking of Eric's Rubik's cube.

"He's gonna keep on us until someone cracks," Eric said, squirting tobacco juice out the window. "This is just the beginning. Maybe we should say something."

Because no one had come forward with a confession or information leading to the arrest and conviction of the gang that had viciously vandalized the ham-radio room, and because Todd had refused to name his attackers, the monks were turning the screws on the student body.

"They learned this shit during the Inquisition," I said. "They've got tons of torture methods. This is only the tip of the iceberg."

"I don't think t-taking away dessert and c-c-closing the rec room qualifies as t-torture," Connor said. "It'll blow over."

"It's the silence stuff that gets me," I said. "Not letting us talk to each other at breakfast and in the dorms and stuff is psychological torture."

"R-relax. They have n-no proof."

"The whole thing is up to Brother Thomas," I said. "It's not Father Gregory. He hasn't said a word. It's not even Brother Thomas's job to come down on us. He's just an English teacher."

Something hit the window. We all flinched, then pressed against the glass, squinting into the darkness. Mary was standing in the grass below, shivering. I pushed Eric out of the way and yanked the window wide open.

"I have to talk to you," she said.

"How'd you know I was in here?"

She pointed to a tall, lone figure in a big grey overcoat retreating down the darkening drive.

"Okay," I whispered. "Go out behind the garden shed. Don't let anyone else see you." I closed the window and watched Todd disappear into Hail Mary Corner.

Eric scowled. "She can't be here. You're going to attract attention."

I ran out the door at half-speed, trying not to look too eager.

TWENTY

CRIMES OF PASSION

Mary stood against the back of the garden shed, fastening the top buttons of her coat, eyes anxious, lips vulnerable. Her hot breath turned to fog in the November chill, reminding me of a dream I'd had a few weeks before but had forgotten until now.

Even though I'd never been there before, I'd dreamed I was in New York City on a bright winter day. Snow was piled everywhere. The trees in Central Park were heavy with white stuff and the pond was a perfectly smooth sheet of ice. Mary and I had the place to ourselves. I remember hugging her and kissing her neck on the shore of the pond. She glanced back at me, amused, and laughed, exhaling a little cloud of vapour. Then she shook her head and skated off across the pond, turning triple axels. Except for the skates, she was completely naked, and so was I, but we didn't notice the cold. Skating after her on wobbly legs, I could never catch up.

Now, in reality, Mary appeared just as beautiful wrapped in a green wool coat and long matching knit scarf. She wasn't smiling, and it looked as if she were about to run away. She wanted to know why I hadn't returned her calls.

"Why should I? Antoine might answer the phone." I reached up and gently touched her face.

"I'm not going out with *André*."

"Well, it sure looked like you were hot for each other at the dance."

"Bill, grow up. He wanted to go out with me again, but I said no. I wanted to be with you. Period."

I let my hand fall from her cheek. "So you say."

"Maybe if you hadn't run away in the middle of the dance, you'd have seen."

"Seen what? You and him dancing to 'Eye of the Tiger'? How could you?"

"I don't know why I'm wasting my time."

"Maybe because André dumped you."

"You're an asshole."

"And you're a slut."

"Goodbye, Bill."

She moved away, but I grabbed her. Her lips were full and her nose was pink and cold. "I think I loved you."

"Let go. I don't want to talk to you anymore. You're in love with yourself."

"You loved me, too."

"Don't kid yourself." She pushed my chest away. "Let go."

I was wearing her down. I could feel it. "Kiss me."

"In your dreams."

"You still love me."

"Bill, let go!"

She struggled a bit, but I pinned her against the wall and kissed her hard, thrusting my tongue into her mouth. I pressed as much of my body against her as I could and slid my thigh between her legs. It was exciting. She let me grope her for a moment, then changed her mind and tried to push me away. I pressed even harder.

"The young lady wants you to let her go—now!" The voice came from the darkness behind the hedge. Brother Thomas's eyes were black and wild. "Are you forcing yourself on her, William?"

Mary and I stood apart, and I felt strangely relieved. *"No!* Are you spying on us?"

Brother Thomas grabbed me by the hair at the back of my head and threw me to the ground. Although my eyes burned, I pretended he hadn't hurt me. I stood and brushed the gravel from my palms.

"Mary?" Brother Thomas said softly.

She considered me with a peculiar mix of anger, pity, and disappointment.

"Is he forcing himself on you, Mary?" Streams of vapour shot out of his nostrils.

"Uh, no, Brother, we were…having a talk." She flicked the hair away from her face.

"Go to the van, Mary. I'm driving you home. For the last time."

She stared at me until I looked away.

When she rounded the corner, Brother Thomas said, "William, you've crossed the line. If you break the rules—"

"The rules break you."

He grabbed me by the collar and pushed me toward the van.

✺

We returned Mary to her parents' split-level. I stayed in the van as Brother Thomas escorted her to the front door. He conferred with her father in the glow of the porch light for what seemed like centuries. Mr. O'Brien peered across the lawn to get a glimpse of me, then slowly nodded. He was fat and looked mad. Mad fat people scared me.

Brother Thomas slammed the door as he got back in the van. "You have no respect for me, this seminary, or that girl. A man is nothing without respect for those around him. You think it's so important to rebel against everything you see, to go your own way. Well, let me tell you something. It's a stronger man who builds something for the benefit of others than a man who tears things down only for himself."

I yawned.

"Everything you do is for self-serving attention." Selfishness is weakness, William. Self-*less*-ness takes real guts. Haven't you learned anything here?" He was expecting an impassioned, emotional response, but he wasn't going to get it.

As we drove back, he struggled to calm himself. We passed the sign at the bottom of the hill—WELCOME TO THE ABBEY AND SEMINARY OF SAINT JOHN THE DIVINE—and then climbed the drive in the dark. We both made an autonomic sign of the cross as we turned into Hail Mary Corner.

"I'm your 'guardian angel,' William. I know you don't like me too much right now, but that's what I am. I believe in you and I'm trying to stop you from wrecking your life. When I was your age, I was lucky enough to have someone hold a mirror up to me. Now I'm returning the favour."

I didn't know whether to laugh or puke.

"Someday," he continued, "you're going to thank me."

"Don't take this the wrong way, Brother, but I wouldn't hold my breath if I were you."

We parked near the gym and sat for a while in the van. The silence was excruciating.

"I know you were the man behind the radio-room break-in," he said. "I want you to own up to it before you leave for home."

Silence.

"What's wrong with you!" His nostrils flared and his lips tightened. "Do you even realize how you were treating that girl?"

Nothing.

"The whole seminary is going crazy," he muttered, exhausted. "Underclassmen assaulting Todd, best friends at each other's throat—"

"Pardon?"

"Well, your little gang. You don't seem to be together anymore. What's going on between you and Jon, anyway? You used to be thick as thieves."

"Why are you always on my case? I don't need a guardian fairy creeping around behind me."

"People have invested things in you, William—their friendship, their trust, their love… All you seem able to repay them with is deceit." He tried to check my reaction, but I twisted away and peered at the empty parking lot. "Look at me!"

Slowly I turned.

"Somehow you ended up being one of the leaders of this school. The running of a school, especially one like ours, has everything to do with the leadership of a few key students. But you're not man enough for the job. After Mass tomorrow, you should leave."

Not man enough. I thought I was going to tip over. He waited for me to explode or to beg forgiveness. All I had were questions. "Tell me about lithium carbonate."

Even in the dark I could see his eyeballs suck a little deeper into their sockets. "What did you say?"

"What's it like to have a nervous breakdown? I looked up lithium carbonate. It's basically for people going insane, isn't it? Do you freak out and babble to yourself? Did you have to go to the nut farm?"

"What are you talking—"

"Now who's jerking whom? C'mon, Brother, we've all made mistakes. You just got wound so tight you snapped. Nineteen seventy-six, wasn't it? If you stop taking lithium, do you freak out again? What if our parents knew we were locked up here with a psycho?"

He hit me on the mouth with the full force of the back of his hand. I was cut, I could feel it, but the surprise was the bigger shock. Fingering my split lip, I glared at him through watery eyes. Now my face really began to burn. I made a move to retaliate, but he blocked it, then smacked me even harder.

When I regained my composure, I said, "You can forget about the dance, your little radio room, and my personal life and I'll forget to tell everyone who hit me and who's insane."

"Get out!"

I couldn't open the door of the van fast enough. He shoved me as hard as he could over and over again, and it felt as if my collarbone might snap. I barely stumbled out before he gunned the engine and sped away.

✤

Gazing up at the picture of Pope John Paul II on the wall of our dorm, I tried to think of something profound to say. The pope was wearing a white mitre and gripping a gold crosier. He offered no more inspiration than his trademark grin, which said, "God, I love my job."

"You told him w-w-*what*?" Connor sputtered, punching me hard on my shoulder where Brother Thomas had shoved me.

"It's over," I said, sitting on my bed. "It got a little out of control. He'll live."

Connor touched my chin just below the cut lip. "You're g-g-gonna need stitches."

"What am I going to tell Father Gregory?"

"I'll tell h-him I h-hit you for being an asshole. He'll b-believe that." I smiled, but it hurt.

"You s-shouldn't have s-s-said anything. What w-were you t-thinking? You were s-supposed to k-keep your yap shut, not try to b-bluff him. You're on y-your own this time."

Eric came in and I rehashed my story for him. He was even less impressed. I watched his face screw up in disgust as I told him. I knew even before he opened his mouth that our friendship had come to an end.

"What's wrong with you, MacAvoy? He gave his life to *God*. I can't believe you."

"Believe it," I said.

Helmut came running in his wool socks, sliding across the floor and losing his balance, nearly taking Connor over with him. "Jon's hurt," he said, picking himself up off the floor. "Someone ran him off Hail Mary Corner."

I ran toward the lights. I ran to Jon.

✤

Between myself and the accident scene there was only darkness. Because I couldn't see the ground beneath me, it felt as if I were flying.

When I arrived at the van, flashlights flickered along the skid marks as kids oohed and ahhed over shattered glass and plastic from the broken headlight and grille. I came to a stop at the edge of the student body whose backs were lit in the glow of the remaining headlight. Gasping, I stared down the road past the end of the headlight beam and into the consuming night.

The rattle of the idling engine and the smell of exhaust filled the air. I tried to see over everyone's shoulders to where Jon was lying on the gravel near the edge of the cliff. I caught a glimpse of Father Gregory's silver hair, then the crowd pressed in again and someone whispered there was something wrong with Jon's head.

Dean tapped my shoulder and aimed his flashlight at where Connor's old bike had gone over the edge and was hanging in a tree, a branch poking through its spokes. Tom Wolosovic pointed out the fact that the keys were still in the van, the door wide open. Connor walked over and turned off the ignition. Brother Thomas was nowhere to be seen.

Brother Fulbert told everyone to take five steps back, but no one budged. He carried a blanket, which he pushed through to Father Gregory, then he started pulling people back by their shoulders. When the crowd finally moved, I saw Jon lying there, his legs sticking out straight, Father Gregory kneeling over him. Jon's eyes were open when Father Gregory flashed the light in them, but he didn't respond when the monk called his name. His hair was dirty and had little bits of dead leaves stuck here and there. His hands and forearms were scraped and bleeding, likely from trying to break his fall. Father Gregory spoke softly to him. There were no more questions, only soothing words of encouragement. As Father Gregory spoke, I told myself Jon was going to be okay, that he didn't look all that bad. Everything would be all right.

The wail of the siren came from out of nowhere. An ambulance snaked its way up the hill, flashing the scene in red. Without a word two medics got out and walked to where Father Gregory knelt over Jon. One medic was pudgy and wore a grey ponytail; the younger one had an earring and a blond moustache. They took great care assessing Jon's condition. The one with the ponytail flashed a light in Jon's eyes as Father Gregory had, then took his pulse. After that he clapped his hands next to Jon's ears. With a pair of scissors, the younger medic cut open Jon's jacket and shirt to inspect his neck, shoulders, and arms.

A police cruiser arrived, siren blaring, and pulled up beside the van. The cop—the same one who had led the desecration investigation—sat inside with the car's dome light on, writing something on a pad of paper.

The ponytailed medic pulled a flat board from the ambulance, then he and his partner gingerly moved Jon onto it. They put a blanket over him and fastened him on with a series of orange belts.

Father Gregory stood, then followed them to the ambulance. The front of his habit was dirty from where he had knelt in the gravel, and it struck me that it was the first time I'd seen such a thing. As he walked past me, he did a double take and reached out for my chin. I had forgotten about my split lip. His eyes were tired and his hand was cold. Without a word Father Gregory stepped into the back of the ambulance and motioned for me to jump in.

I sat on the floor at Jon's feet, next to Father Gregory. The younger medic crawled past us and knelt over Jon. He took off his jacket as his partner sealed the doors behind us. When the ambulance lurched into gear, the medic braced himself, then smoothed his moustache with the back of his wrist. He looked around the cramped space and gestured to an empty spot on top of the wheel well where one of us could sit. Father Gregory nodded to me, and I took the seat where I could see Jon's face. His eyes were now closed and his head was unnaturally rigid in a thick foam brace. All expression was erased from his face; there weren't any dreams.

As we rolled down the hill, Todd led the group of onlookers in the recitation of a Hail Mary. Out the back window dozens of hands flashed red in the brake lights as they made the sign of the cross in perfect unison. *In the name of the Father, the Son, and the Holy Spirit*. They prayed for Jon and for Brother Thomas, wherever he was.

TWENTY ONE

SACRIFICE

My nerves were killing me. My appetite had vanished and I was beginning to lose weight. The acid that bubbled continuously in my chest wouldn't respond to Rolaids. I felt a colony of zits teeming under the soft blond hairs of my chin. Above that my lip throbbed warmly, though it was finally starting to heal. Everything else, however, was getting worse.

Jon had been in a coma for six days and had been flown in a helicopter to Vancouver General Hospital. His head injury was "considerable," and it kept the doctors guessing. I focused on the fact that, aside from the scrapes on his hands and forearms, the rest of him had looked fine. When they parked Jon in the emergency room of Saint Crispin's Hospital in Ennis, I had stood in the hall staring at the soles of his feet, waiting for something to happen. I waited a long time. Finally the doctor pulled the curtain shut and I never saw Jon again.

The next day every candle in the abbey church was ablaze and a novena was begun. Jon's name was mentioned at Mass, vespers, and rosary and before each meal. His clothes were left in his wardrobe and his papers remained in his desk as symbols of his imminent return. I spent every available moment in prayer; everyone else tried to get back to normal.

Connor was too busy to spend time with me. He was already preparing for his transformation. Because his last name was Atkins, he was about to become the Junior Senior. His duties would commence after Christmas break and include shadowing the Senior Senior, learning the ropes of house monitoring, and eventually alternating days of responsibility. In addition to ensuring a seamless transfer of power from one year to the next, this tradition also afforded the Senior Senior extra time to study for the finals.

Eric treated me like Contagion. I was the carrier of the doubting disease with which he had become infected.

Todd maintained a low profile after the ambush, yet he didn't carry an air of defeat. He absorbed what had happened to him—the humiliation, the hate—and had internalized it somehow. Housework wasn't such a big deal, he seemed to conclude. After all, he was graduating in six months. What did he care? While he physically remained at Saint John's, his spirit had passed to the real world.

Michael Ashbury continued to wear his hockey gloves and use his goalie stick during Sunday Morning Sheet Exchange. But he wasn't flaunting it. His growing self-confidence was born not of revenge but emancipation.

No one saw Brother Thomas again that year. All we were told was that he had left the monks to stay with his real brother in Winnipeg and recuperate. His classes were reassigned to other monks. There was an Extraordinary Meeting of the Student Council to discuss the matter. Father Gregory said Brother Thomas had been overstressed for some time and that the accident at Hail Mary Corner had caused him tremendous remorse and confusion. No one ever mentioned the attic break-and-enter again. I suppose we should have felt relieved.

Mary wouldn't return my calls, and that left me numb.

It was now Saturday, two weeks before the end of the term. At breakfast Father Gregory asked for volunteers to help slaughter chickens down at the farm. I had never killed a chicken before and couldn't imagine why anyone would be willing to give up a Saturday morning to do it.

The farm felt like another country. Here, just beyond the orchard at the far side of Mount Saint John, you couldn't see the bell tower or the wings of the seminary and monastery stretching out to the heavens above and to the souls in the valley below.

I was the only junior to volunteer. Todd was there, as well as a couple of curious, giggling grade eighters in old shirts and overalls. They were throwing rocks at the chicken coop. Although I had been aware of them for almost four months, I didn't know their names. But I did remember their faces, especially since the attack on Todd. They both had bright eyes and the remnants of baby fat. They said their names were Frank and Brendan. I picked up a rock and threw it at them.

"Stop tormenting those birds!" I ordered.

Brendan hopped and nearly fell as he dodged the rock. "We're just having fun," he whined.

"Fun? Don't you eat chicken?"

"Yeah," Frank said, puffing out his chest a little.

"You think it comes from the supermarket in one of those neat little white foam trays with a little Kotex thingy to catch all the blood, don't you?"

"No, we don't," Brendan said.

"Well, good. It's important to take part in killing your food once in a while. Brings it all back into perspective. We're hungry, they're the food. Forget Safeway. It's just a bird, a block, an axe, and *whack!*"

"Leave 'em alone, Bill," Brother Simon said. He was in charge of the orchard, nine sheep, twelve cows, over two hundred chickens, and everything else that had to do with Saint John's nearly self-sufficient farm.

"I'm just razzin' them, Brother."

"Well, smart guy, you can show 'em how it's done."

For a farmer Brother Simon seemed thin and fragile. His hands, however, were huge and he had fingers like thick sausages. He also had the best hair of all the monks—kind of an Elvis Presley thing, circa the 1968 comeback TV special. He only wore his habit in church. The rest of the time he dressed like a farmer. Brother Simon never talked down to us. It wasn't in him. Unfortunately he was always out at the barn, away from the student body. It seemed like such a waste.

His real name, the one he had before taking his vows, was Leslie Postlethwaite. Kids teased him about it every chance they got, but he laughed it off. I'm sure he thanked the Lord every day for helping him trade up to his new, more masculine name.

Brother Simon led us into the ammonia-reeking pen and grabbed "the stick"—a long metal wire with a little hook at the end. Frank and Brendan were impressed when he sliced it through the air. The white mob of feathers screamed and ran to the other side of the pen.

"Simple," Brother Simon instructed. "You just grab 'em by the feet like this." He hooked one, lifted it, and removed it from its clan. "You have to be careful not to injure the others. If you accidentally cut one and the others see blood, they'll peck at the wounded bird, sometimes to death."

"You're kidding," Todd said.

"They also do this to birds with birth defects. They look for any weakness and attack."

"Their own kind?" Brendan asked.

"You got it," Brother Simon said.

I grabbed the chicken off the wire and held it flapping upside down. This was nothing like hunting. I felt like a murderer. Brother Simon fished out two more birds and then we went outside.

Todd was stoking a fire under a barrel of boiling water. Brother Simon had sharpened a machete and left it on a big block of wood. "You aim to chop the head off with the first blow," the monk explained. "It's the only humane way. You get squeamish and miss, chop half the neck, they get hurt and die an agonizing death. Get it?"

Everyone nodded.

"Okay, pay attention. Bill, you first."

I handed the legs of my chicken to Brendan, took hold of the soft comb, and steadied the neck on the chopping block. I raised the machete, stopped in midair, and looked around at my accomplices.

"Make the first one count," Brother Simon said.

Whack! Blood sprayed, and a strangled gurgling came from the headless, flapping body. I tossed the head onto the grass to await a hundred and fifty of its closest friends. Brendan tossed the body into a wire pen. It jumped and bashed itself around, trying to fly.

"Now," Brother Simon said, "you've heard the saying 'running around like a chicken with its head cut off,' haven't you?" We nodded. "Well, here it is in the flesh. Take a good look." We looked. "Go ahead and laugh if you have to. Get it over with. But then let's try to show some respect. They're God's creatures and they're dying so we can live."

Wide-eyed with excitement, Frank and Brendan each tried with their own birds and did well. Todd began dipping the bodies in the boiling vat so that plucking the feathers would be a snap. Brother Simon put the bloody machete back in my hand and arranged us in a production line before getting into his truck and driving away. He left his dog, a Border collie named Remus, to watch over us.

Remus's teeth had been worn down to nubs from years of nipping at the heels of cattle. He was suspicious of everyone, except Brother Simon, and was particularly leery of our doings this day. Remus was one of only two pups to survive the litter, and his twin brother had died last year. Broken hip. Rumour was that Brother Simon had cried the day he had to put poor Romulus down.

As each man became familiar with his task, we gradually picked up speed. I put the blade to neck after skinny neck, giving it everything I had. *Whack, gurgle, flap-flap. Whack, gurgle, flap-flap.* I set the rhythm and then became a slave to it, sickening myself when I realized I liked it.

"It's like the French Revolution," Brendan observed. "Do you think they know they're about to die?"

"Well," I said, wiping blood on my overalls, "they're basically stupid, but they know something's up when you separate them from the others. You can see it in their eyes when you stretch them out on the block. They seem calm, almost peaceful right before you let them have it. You'd think they'd fight all the way to the end."

Frank and Brendan stared at me, blinking.

Whack! I tossed another head onto the pile, then had to sit down. My eyes were burning.

Frank crouched beside me. "Bill, you all right?"

"No."

Brendan walked over and put a nervous hand on my shoulder. I bowed my head and cried, covering my face with bloody hands and sobbing so hard I couldn't catch my breath.

✴

After the job was done, Frank and Brendan went up to shower. Todd and I stayed behind to dispose of the feathers, guts, and heads. Brother Simon returned to collect the bodies and told us to douse the pile of discards with gasoline and torch it before we left. "It'll stink to high heaven if you don't," he warned.

We splashed a few gallons of gas on the carnage and piled on some dry branches, then—like kids around a birthday cake—debated who would get to light the mess. When I realized what we were doing, I told Todd to go ahead and do the honours. He grabbed a match and hesitated, then tossed the box to me. "We'll do it at the same time."

Todd lit his match one-handed with his thumbnail. It was a cool move, but not nearly as great as he thought. It reminded me of the way he had cut the deck of cards in the Casino a couple of months back. We tossed our matches in unison. The white, red, and yellow heap whooshed into a napalmlike inferno.

"Feeling a little lonely these days?" Todd asked.

"*No.* Get beat up by any anklebiters lately?"

Todd didn't lash back. He simply gazed into the fire.

"Sorry," I said. "I'm a little touchy."

"I noticed. So did a hundred and fifty chickens." Todd probed the bubbling pile with a stick. "Jon's going to be all right, you know."

"We couldn't believe it when the anklebiters jumped you. Man, that was weird. We were practising onstage, not thinking twice about them. It was like one of those gang attacks you hear about in public schools in places like Detroit."

Todd didn't say anything.

"But I came out looking worse than you did." I touched the five stitches on my lip with a less-than-sterile pinkie.

"Connor sure popped you a good one. Did you nail him, too?"

"Yeah, just in the gut. But you don't get scars from that." Connor and I were so good at convincing everyone about our fictional fight that we had started believing it ourselves.

"At least it was just one guy," Todd said. "And I'm sure you and Connor will end up being friends again. Plus you've got Eric, too." He tossed his poker into the growing pyre. "Believe it or not, I never wanted to be Senior Senior. It just made everything a million times worse." The burning guts popped and hissed. "I've never been invited to the cliff or the store—or even for a walk down the stinking drive. Not once." Todd looked through the heat shimmer with accusing eyes. "You think anyone ever tells me their secrets? Or wants to know mine? Not even the other seniors. When you spend all your time alone, you get to see things clearly. And I see I've wasted my time. I don't have one friend to show for four years in this dump. Four years, Bill."

We watched the heads and feathers melt into a black-and-red ooze. Remus loped over and sat between us. The dog looked at the fire, then up at Todd and me. He kept his head down and ears drawn back, as if his earlier suspicions had been fully, tragically, confirmed.

✳

That evening after dinner I called Mary to tell her I was sorry and that I missed her. But when she answered the phone my throat was so tight I couldn't speak. She said hello a few more times, and I was sure she knew it was me. I tried to speak again, but my tongue wouldn't budge, and she finally hung up.

I clicked off the light in the phone booth and sat cocooned in darkness. After a few minutes, I heard music. Connor and Eric were jamming in the rec room without me. I felt nauseated, dizzy, then fled the booth and ran upstairs. In the dorm I grabbed my coat and guitar case and struck out into the night.

Moonlight bathed the fields and trees in silver. The world was getting cold. My ears stung as I trudged past the naked metal posts where the soccer net used to hang. I walked along the trail leading around the Bog, past the black silhouette of Our Lady of the Lake, and eventually ended up on the far bank. I stared out over flat, lifeless water. The ice that had formed along the shore framed a scattering of stars, a mirror of the black December night. I paused for a moment, taking it all in, then set my guitar case down and lit a cigarette.

Eventually I took the guitar out and tried to play it, but the cold sent the strings out of tune. The notes echoed sourly across the Bog, and I couldn't make them right. Finally I gave up and held the guitar aloft, considering it from every angle. Then, in a moment of inspiration, I bent and gently launched it like a toy boat into the rippling stars.

TWENTY TWO

SIGNS OF PEACE

The abbey church was festooned with fragrant cedar boughs and the purple bunting of Advent. Bright spikes of flame danced on thick columnar candles, and islands of red-hot poinsettias blazed around the altar. The place looked warm and inviting, but my nose was running from the cold. On top of my uniform I wore my winter coat, scarf, and gloves. This was Sunday Mass, and although Christmas was just around the corner, the monks wouldn't turn up the heat. They would only splurge if the plumbing was in danger of bursting.

Todd was at the main entrance, greeting members of the laity as they came trickling in. Eric shuffled around in his altar-boy robes as if he'd rather be anyplace other than here. He used to perform this task—this holy service—with solemn, serious piety. Now he merely went through the motions. Connor sat at the other end of the pew next to Dean, while I knelt alone on callused knees. As we watched the church slowly come to life, Father Albert crossed in

195

front of the altar, bowed, and headed into the confessional. I got up, made the sign of the cross, and followed him in.

Father Albert preferred the informal face-to-face Confession style instead of the anonymous closet method. So did I. Kneeling behind a screen in the dark was for the weak. Why even bother?

When I entered the warm little room, Father Albert was yawning and rubbing his eyes. "See why I like hiding in here?" He moved his chair closer to the baseboard heater. He wore his cowl over his head and his face was cast in shadow. "Sit down, Bill. In the name of the Father, the Son, and the Holy Spirit. May God help you make a good Confession."

"Forgive me, Father, for I have sinned. It's been two months since my last Confession."

"I'm honoured," he said, brushing the crumbs of Sunday breakfast from the lap of his habit.

I told him the usual. The thing I refused to get up and parade in front of everyone at weekday Mass. The thing he'd heard a million times before from every hormone-intoxicated kid on the hill. The Sin of Onan. I told him I had it under control, that my prayers had finally been answered, but then it had come back like a curse. He yawned some more and squinted his I'm-trying to-be-serious eyes.

I told him I was the one who had arranged the Ennis High gig and had convinced everyone else to go, and that I had invaded the cloister and the ham-radio room. At that point Father Albert started waking up. I told him I had taken Mary's virginity and had been rough with her behind the gym, that I had lost control of myself and wasn't a gentleman. That made him sit up straight. Finally I told him I had betrayed the trust of a friend, that I was responsible for Brother Thomas's breakdown and Jon's coma. He reached up and pushed the cowl off his head. "Explain."

"I told Brother Thomas he was crazy and reminded him of his problem—being manic-depressive and all. And then I made him hit me. See?" I fingered the thin pink scar. "That's when he took off in the van."

"How did you know? And how could you do it, especially if you knew he was sick?"

"Because I'm mean, Father. I'm evil."

In all the time I had known Father Albert I had never seen him disappointed in me. Now that and much more were apparent in his face. I felt worthless and small.

"Information is a powerful weapon," he said finally. "Brother Thomas has a medical problem that can affect his personality. You knew that. You hurt him with what you knew. And this other trust you broke—tell me about that."

"I can't, Father."

"Why not?"

"I'd just be doing it all over again."

Father Albert's face turned grey. "We've all been praying very hard, but Jon's condition hasn't improved. I'm sure I'm not telling you anything you don't already know... As it stands, we've lost Brother Thomas for the semester. We could lose Jon forever." He stopped for a moment to loosen his collar, then leaned back in his chair. "You've put me in an awkward position. If we were outside the confessional, you know you'd be expelled."

"I can't go back to Calgary, Father. I just can't."

He waited.

"I'm *nothing* there. I have no friends. My family's falling apart. I'll be completely alone. I can't, Father."

"You still think this whole thing's about you. Listen to yourself. It's all *you*, isn't it?"

I bowed my head.

"You've dug a deep hole for yourself. You need to pull some of that dirt back in with you in order to climb out." He took a deep breath. "You're not evil, but you're being selfish. And selfishness leads to loneliness."

The first strains of the processional hymn bled through the walls. It was a rare Sunday when Father Albert wasn't in command of the musical liturgy. He leaned forward and held my hands. His fingers were trembling. "You've confessed your sins and that's the start of the healing process. God's forgiven you. Now it's time to try to forgive yourself. For your penance..." He pushed back, looked at the ceiling, then glanced at me again. "You're an adult now. Only you can decide what needs to be done, but before you do anything I want you to watch *Ben-Hur*. There's a copy on Beta in the library. Just fast-forward through the commercials."

"What does *Ben-Hur* have to do with any of this?"

"Everything. It's a classic. I'm the priest here. Do as you're told."

"Yes, Father."

"Now go in peace to love and serve the Lord. Say an Act of Contrition before Communion and offer up your prayers for Jon. Mass is about to start. In the name of the Father, the Son, and the Holy Spirit. Amen." He got up and placed his hands on my head for a moment of blessing. "Don't carry all that guilt around with you. Make it right, then leave it behind."

After he left, I put my hands on the heater and held them there until I thought they were going to fry.

✳

Three-quarters of the way through Mass the abbot told the congregation to offer one another the Sign of Peace. The monks didn't like it. They called it a "post-Vatican II, touchy-feely" thing. I always thought of it as a sort of seventh-inning stretch. Tom Wolosovic turned around and gave me a weak, perfunctory handshake. Seeing the haunted look in my eyes, Dean reached out and took my hand. He shook it warmly and said, *"Pax vobiscum."*

I noticed Michael Ashbury, his Sunday hair smoothed flat against his skull, sitting in the back row at the end of the pew with three other underclassmen. Todd stood behind him in his official usher sash. Michael rose and took a step toward Todd, offering his hand in peace. The hand was ignored as Todd busied himself arranging baskets for the collection.

At the end of the Eucharistic prayer Michael and four of his classmates went up to the altar to help distribute Communion. Each received a gold ciborium and took a spot along the front of the altar facing the congregation. They waited for the lines to form as the towering organ pipes churned out contemplative accompaniment. I sat down.

Whenever I chose to abstain from Communion, I felt like a speed bump on the road to God. The pews were so close everyone had to step over or around me in order to make their way to the altar. Helmut, Dean, and Connor brushed past my knees. I was the only one left behind.

I watched Mary, her fat father, and her family shuffle by in a prayerful procession. She wore a blue dress, powder-blue eye shadow, and no panty hose. She must have been freezing. She tried hard not to look my way but eventually granted me a smile.

As the stream of faithful dried up, one by one Michael's classmates took their empty ciboria back to the abbot at the altar. The ushers were always the last to receive Communion and Todd was the last of the ushers. Jaw set, gaze locked, Todd approached the steps where Michael waited alone.

Although Michael was on the second step leading up to the altar, he was still dwarfed by the Senior Senior. He held out the thin white wafer, but Todd neither presented his hands to receive nor opened his mouth to have it placed on his tongue. I could see Michael's lips say "The Body of Christ" as he waited for Todd to acknowledge him. Frozen, they stared at each other for a long moment. People were starting to notice. The organ fell silent and a few muffled coughs echoed from deep in the congregation. Finally Todd bowed his head and presented his hands—palms up, one cradling the other. "Amen," he said, and Michael placed the Blessed Sacrament in the outstretched hand. Todd put the host in his mouth, made the sign of the cross, and sealed the truce between them.

That afternoon, alone in the seniors' classroom, I watched *Ben-Hur*—an epic tale of friendship betrayed. Just as the tape finished rewinding, the Angelus rang through the cold slate sky. And as the student body marched off to dinner, chattering about Christmas ski vacations and next week's final exams, I went up and packed my things, called a cab, and quietly left Saint John's for good.

TWENTY THREE

EPILOGUE
September 2001

The hotel isn't far off the highway, and I can hear the intermittent drone of traffic, mostly eighteen-wheelers on the overnight run. I study the cottage-cheese ceiling and wonder if that's asbestos stuck up there, and if it is, what the effects will be from breathing it all night. Then I take a deep pull on my Marlboro Light.

I lie in a king-size bed tallying the nights I've slept alone since getting married: five in almost three years. I figure if I don't actually sleep tonight I'll still be holding at four. I wonder if Emily is awake, then reach for the phone to call and tell her I love her, that I feel awkward and very much alone.

A few days ago a package arrived with an audiocassette tape and a letter from Jon's mother. The letter explained that she stumbled upon some old boxes when they sold their house to move into a new condominium. One of the boxes had belonged to Jon. Inside, she discovered the tape with my name on it. It was a name, she said, she hadn't seen or heard in a very long time. She thought the tape might contain private things that might mean something to me.

I recognized the tape immediately. I had recorded it in the summer of 1982 before my last semester at the Seminary of Saint John the Divine. I remember sending it to Jon toward the end of that summer, and although he recorded a reply, it was too late to mail it back. He forgot to bring it with him when he came to the seminary that year and eventually forgot about it completely. When it arrived in the mail nearly twenty years later, I couldn't listen to it right away. I had to prepare myself, go back, earn the right to hear it.

Rolling over, I turn on the light, slip the cassette into my Walkman, and pull the earphones over my head. I lie back and place the Walkman on my chest. The voice reminds me of one of my students last year, one of the troublemakers who made me question, just for a moment, if I'm in the right line of work.

The tape was recorded in my old room at my parents' house. I can hear the dog barking in the backyard. I tell Jon how much I hate Calgary and being away from the seminary. I tell him about my crappy summer job at the grocery store and the movies I've seen. I'm writing a story, "The Night of the Bog Monster," and I just might let him read it someday. At the very end, and only with great effort, I tell him I miss having him around.

Jon's reply fills Side B. He says he had a dream about me, and then this tape arrived the very next day. He lists the Beatles tunes he's learning to play and even gives me a taste of a drum solo, which makes me laugh out loud. He tells me about *Helter Skelter*, the book he's been reading, and says only an idiot like Charlie Manson could twist great lyrics like that. Later that week, he mentions, he's going to get his learner's permit and go for a very long drive.

When the news of his summer comes to an end, Jon says he thinks about me all the time. No one else understands him. There are a million things to tell me when we get together. Just hearing my voice makes him feel better, not so alone. He's in the middle of telling me about his top score in Asteroids when the machine snaps off and lies silent on my skin.

✳

Between my elbows the pattern of aquamarine stars has worn off the white Formica, revealing the dark brown laminate below. Suddenly a plate of toasted white bread and a mug of see-through coffee slides into view. I sit up straight. There isn't any jam and I'm not about to bother the overworked waitress, so I just butter the toast and dunk it in. At least I have a booth.

I spent a lot of time over an ironing board and in front of a mirror this morning, suddenly struck by the fear that I wasn't properly dressed. But what did it matter? After all, I wasn't going to a funeral; I was merely going back up the hill. Nevertheless, I shaved with a fresh blade and spit-shined my shoes.

As I eat breakfast, I watch other people come and go: a young family on a last-minute summer vacation, a salesman driving between territories. The Maple Diner is still the only show on this side of Ennis. It catches all the southbound traffic, fresh from the pass, and the empty logging trucks heading north. Occasionally, on the way back from town, Jon and I would nip in here for milk shakes.

There really isn't time for this visit. I'm supposed to be preparing for the start of classes, organizing an entirely new study plan. Plus, I've been given some administrative duties that are taking up a lot of extra time. After I got the tape, I told Emily everything, held nothing back. Making this trip, I said, was something I thought I should do. She kissed me and said it was something I absolutely had to do.

✳

After breakfast I drive up the seminary road, reacquainting myself with the series of straight climbs and switchbacks lined with spruce, grass, and the occasional blush of flowers. Soon I find myself at Hail Mary Corner.

Although there are several sharp turns as the road snakes its way uphill, only one has earned a name. The day after the end of World

War II there was a fatal accident here. The road had been freshly paved and rerouted to give better access to two new buildings on the north side of the property. Unfortunately it also produced a blind corner on a cliff that drops thirty feet into the woods below.

On that rainy afternoon a truck swinging wide through the turn forced an oncoming car to swerve off the pavement, sending it flying over the little cliff and into the trees below. Something—the hand of God, we were told—reached out and saved everyone, except the little boy sitting in back. Somehow the kid must have slipped through His fingers.

The following Sunday the monks and seminarians came down in an orderly procession, the abbot and altar boys leading everyone to the turn. They made the sign of the cross, read scripture, sprinkled holy water, and otherwise anointed the spot for the protection of future travellers. The whole affair is said to have ended with the recitation of the Hail Mary, which everyone was encouraged to repeat when approaching the turn. Since that time there had been plenty of near misses, but no one was hurt...until Jon and Brother Thomas.

Almost twenty years have passed since I last travelled this road, and still there are no markers urging SLOW or CAUTION for the benefit of the uninitiated—only the invisible signpost that announces I'm about to cross the threshold from the real world into a place apart. I say no prayer.

*

The abbey church is the only thing as big as I remember it. The moment I slip inside and out of the sunlight I'm struck by the realization that I haven't entered God's House in a long time. The place is dead except for a ruby rack of flickering candles and Brother Ambrose, who intercepts me before I can sit down. Other than that his hair is lighter and his skin a little thinner, he essentially looks the same. I catch a whiff of his cooking-oil smell as he gives me a big bear hug. Then he gives me the news.

He tells me that Jon died that Christmas Eve of 1982, which I already knew, and that the abbot passed away a week later, which I hadn't heard. Father Gregory was elected to take his place, and still serves as abbot. Father Albert is outside, past the holly bushes, under a cool green blanket in the cemetery. He was called home with a heart attack about four years ago. Brother Ambrose tells me I should stop and pay my respects.

After graduating from Saint John the Divine, Connor took intensive speech therapy to overcome his stutter and went on to study languages at university. The government snapped him up and put him in an Arabic immersion program. He served as a translator for the Canadian Forces during the Gulf War and distinguished himself as a leader. Eric became a securities trader in Toronto. He had twins—and his marriage was annulled. No one knew much about Todd. Rumour was that he became a carpenter in upstate New York. Michael Ashbury was the only one of us to receive Holy Orders. Taking the name Brother David, he made his preliminary vows and was a novitiate at the abbey. If I stick around, Brother Ambrose says, I can see him after vespers.

It feels right that Michael Ashbury has a new name. He's no longer the kid I once knew. When I hear the old names spoken of in new contexts, I'm not sure how to react. Their owners are gone as I knew them, replaced with something else. And yet no matter what they've become, I knew them in the becoming. That makes us kin forever.

※

The library is completely new, with carpeting throughout. Things are a lot cushier than I recall. The old wooden shelves that supported the books are gone, and beige metal shelving now dominates the bright, airy space. The card files have also vanished. In their place two computer terminals sit on a table next to the first row of shelves. They wait, cursors blinking, for students looking for answers.

I can't find him at first, then I spot him with an open book. He's leaning against the frame of a floor-to-ceiling window, gazing out over Ennis Valley. Brother Thomas looks small—he seems to be shrinking—but in the morning light he appears luminous and content.

He doesn't seem the least bit surprised to see me.

"Brother?"

"William MacAvoy—Man of God, you've grown."

Hundreds of students have passed between us, and he doesn't miss a beat. He walks over and gives me a sincere handshake, one of those "I really mean it" double-handed jobs.

"How tall are you?" he asks.

"Six-one. Shot up in college."

"It suits you."

"How are things with you, Brother?"

"Grand, grand. It's been a long time, hasn't it? You look…more substantial. I have to say I never expected to see you again."

"Likewise," I say. "But here I am."

"How has life treated you, William?"

"Good. Got married three years back."

"Congratulations. I won't even ask about kids. You don't have the look about you. Are you gainfully employed?"

"I'm teaching," I say. "High-school English."

"Wonders never cease. Written anything lately?"

It's remarkable how twenty years of maturity can unravel and coil around your ankles in a matter of seconds. As I fumble for the first lines of the speech I've been rehearsing, I begin to feel as if coming back has been a terrible mistake. "What's new with you?"

"This," he says, gesturing to the whole room. Then his eye catches the new computers. "We're modernizing, William. They call us a medieval anachronism, but we can spot a deal on IBM clones when we see one. The computers make everything faster and more efficient. Let me show you the new system."

He sits at one of the computers and continues. "We can find a book instantly by inputting the subject, title, or author's name. The computer also helps us keep track of where everything is. Each year more and more people rely on this library. And I'm not just talking about students. You're sitting in one of the greatest religious and philosophy collections in the Pacific Northwest. We've made a career out of adapting the past to solve today's problems. Whatever the current crisis happens to be—but listen to me. I don't mean to preach." He looks at me to check my reaction, then gets up. "Go ahead, try it."

I sit at the terminal as Brother Thomas pulls up another chair. "Brother, I need to talk to you about something."

"I'm listening."

"The reason I came up here after all these years is to see you. I came to say I'm sorry."

"Sorry for what?" He reaches over and begins typing something on the keyboard in front of me.

"Well, for saying all that stuff to you before…before you went away to visit your brother that year."

"What *stuff* was that?"

"What I said to you in the van before you took off, before Jon's accident at Hail Mary Corner."

He clears the screen and returns the blinking cursor. He has found the file I've been looking for. "William, I have to tell you something. Even though there's no way to make amends, I apologized to Jon's parents after I returned. But for the life of me I still can't remember anything about that accident. I don't even have a complete memory of the week leading up to it. I've been on medication for years. I don't mind telling people that now. That was my second break-down and I haven't had another since. Not a day goes by that I don't think about that boy."

"So you don't remember us talking in the van, any of the things I said to you?"

"Most of that year seems foggy to me. Things have been much better since I changed my prescription. Should *I* be apologizing for something?"

"No, Brother."

"Well, then, what did you want to talk about?"

"I want you to forgive me for what I said to you that night."

His brow creases, the lines noticeably sharper. "You really believe you're to blame for my breakdown, for my running down Jon? It was an accident, William. An accident I'm fully responsible for. I was careless with my medication and I was careless with my driving. Don't take this the wrong way, but I don't think—"

"Trust me. I remember exactly what happened."

He pushes away from the terminal. "So you want me to make things better? Is that what you're getting at? Well, I can't forgive you because I don't even remember having the conversation. I'm afraid you'll have to forgive yourself. I can't do it for you. If you want something done right..."

"Memory's a tricky thing, William. Sometimes what we remember as being so important—the things we can't forget—really aren't such a big deal, after all. The last thing I remember about you before the accident was...let me see." He folds his arms and gazes heavenward. "You were playing guitar with your band, and you weren't half bad. You played Beatles tunes, didn't you?"

"Yeah."

"Well, that's it then. That's the last thing I remember. You guys had a funny name, right? Something cheeky. What was it?"

I look up and tug my chin as if I'm trying to remember.

"Let's go for a walk later," he says. "I'm supposed to meet with one of our new staff members. We're hiring civilians these days to fill in the gaps."

He glances at his watch. "It's twenty after ten. He'll be here any minute. I really should be going."

"Ten-twenty," I repeat, as if it could be anything else.

It's amazing how often that number appears in my life. To everyone else it's an innocuous thing, something devoid of all but numeric meaning. No matter where I am or what I'm doing, each time I come across it I'm reminded of Jon. He left me an inescapable souvenir.

"The library looks great, Brother. You should see the abbot about a raise."

"Bring your wife up sometime. We'd love to meet her."

"I will, Brother. See you after lunch." I turn to walk away.

Before I reach the door my body stiffens. I stop and turn to face him. "I loved Jon, you know."

Brother Thomas looks up without judgement or condemnation. "I know."

"But he never knew it."

"Well, William, now he does."

✳

Inside our old classroom the urge to touch overwhelms me: door-knobs, desktops, chalk, well-nibbled pencils, the contents of shelves and drawers. As I rediscover those things temporarily misplaced, I find myself trusting the wisdom of my hands over the less intimate senses.

I open and close what could have been my desk. I run a finger across initials carved into the windowsill, then lean over and spit into Eric's Copenhagen bush below. I walk over and remove the yellowed palm frond from behind the crucifix above the chalk-board. Some unknown student placed it there on Palm Sunday only six months ago. I tuck it into my breast pocket, then pull the door closed behind me.

The thud of my shoes on the terrazzo floor is heavier, more assured. It doesn't sound right at all. I walk past the other class-rooms and then finally downstairs to the students' chapel. My hand automatically reaches for the holy water, but the font has gone dry. The air is stale as I stand in the doorway, staring at where we all used to rub rosary beads, where Jon tried to tell me what he felt. I go to one of the windows and fight with a latch that has seized shut over the summer months. Forcing it open with the heel of my hand, I let the fresh breeze wash over me.

I take the last few steps to our pew, genuflect, and then kneel in Jon's place for a while. It is here on tender knees that I realize I'll be bringing back neither forgiveness nor absolution. Instead I will leave something behind.

Now, when I reach into that top drawer of my mind, that place where I keep my most cherished regrets, I find an empty space. It is the room I save for peace.

MORE NEW FICTION FROM BEACH HOLME

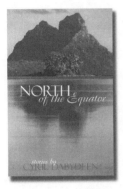

North of the Equator
by Cyril Dabydeen
SHORT FICTION $18.95 CDN $14.95 US ISBN: 0-88878-423-6

Cyril Dabydeen's new collection of stories, *North of the Equator*, looks at the polarities of tropical and temperate places. Acclaimed novelist Sam Selvon (*The Lonely Londoners*) says, "Dabydeen is in the vanguard of contemporary short-story writers, shuttling with equal and consummate skill from rural Guyana to metropolitan Canada." Dabydeen's characters live in limbo, stretched between two worlds: one, an adopted home in Canada; the other, a birthplace in the islands scattered across the equator.

Cold Clear Morning
by Lesley Choyce
NOVEL $18.95 CDN $14.95 US ISBN: 0-88878-416-3

After the death of his high-school sweetheart, Taylor Colby has returned to his roots to live once again with his noble but isolated boat-builder father in a coastal Nova Scotia village. Complicating matters further, Taylor's mother, who has been battling cancer, attempts to reconcile with both her husband and son whom she deserted decades earlier. As Taylor grapples with family dysfunction, he becomes involved with Jillian, a feminist professor from Philadelphia, and her troubled twelve-year-old son, who are on the run.

Tending the Remnant Damage
by Sheila Peters
SHORT FICTION $18.95 CDN $14.95 US ISBN: 0-88878-417-1

Sheila Peters creates people who often feel out of sync with the spiritual, emotional, and physical environments they find themselves in. Two old people on a farm try to comprehend the inevitable fate befalling them, all the while contemplating the strange goings-on of neighbours. A young woman on the lam from Texas finds herself beached in the Queen Charlottes on her way to Alaska. Their universe is our universe, but with a twist that makes it refreshingly new and decidedly different.

BEACH HOLME PUBLISHING ♦ WWW.BEACHHOLME.BC.CA